LIFELINE

A WARRIOR'S CRY FOR HELP

LIFELINE

A WARRIOR'S CRY FOR HELP

ERIC QUINTANILLA

Halo
PUBLISHING
INTERNATIONAL

Halo Publishing International
7550 WIH-10 #800, PMB 2069,
San Antonio, TX 78229

First Edition, May 2023
ISBN: 978-1-63765-393-7
Library of Congress Control Number: 2023905086

Halo Publishing International is a self-publishing company that publishes adult fiction and non-fiction, children's literature, self-help, spiritual, and faith-based books. We continually strive to help authors reach their publishing goals and provide many different services that help them do so. We do not publish books that are deemed to be politically, religiously, or socially disrespectful, or books that are sexually provocative, including erotica. Halo reserves the right to refuse publication of any manuscript if it is deemed not to be in line with our principles. Do you have a book idea you would like us to consider publishing? Please visit www. halopublishing.com for more information.

I would first like to thank God because, with his help and guidance, I overcame my darkest days. I next want to thank my amazing wife, Alanna. Without her love, patience, attentiveness, and guidance, I would not have accomplished everything I have today. I also want to thank my children, Logan, Jami, and Alexis. You all encourage me to be a better father and person. To my parents, Martha and Tino, and my brother, Joel, you all laid the foundations, established my morals, and gave me the guidance that made me into the man I am today.

To my brothers and sisters in arms, you are never alone. To those with whom I've deployed and served, all of you have impacted me in more ways than you will ever know. I will always cherish the good times and bad times, but, most importantly, the laughter and tears we shared.

Lastly, to De. Thank you for pushing me to keep writing, offering feedback, and convincing me to publish this book. I am truly grateful.

Chapter 1

A flash of lightning and a crack of thunder echoes through the night sky, jolting Mike awake. He feels the beads of sweat running down the sides of his temples and a cold chill down his spine. His heart races, his chest tightens, and his mouth is dry. He rapidly scans the room, desperately trying to regain his surroundings. Quickly, he sits on the side of the bed, feet planted firmly on the floor, and his comforting twitch helps to center him and remind him he is safe, far away from the horrors that haunt his nightmares. Nightmares—that's an understatement. Burying his face in his hands, he feels the faint taste of blood crest through his lips. The bitter taste of iron fills his mouth, oozing from the rawness inside his cheek. Looking at the other side of the bed, his heart melts.

An overwhelming sense of calmness crashes over Mike. But then a new fear overcomes him—is this a dream or reality? A soft moan fills the room as she gently repositions in bed. *This can't be happening,* Mike thinks to himself as he carefully and gently runs his hand along the curves of her body, careful not to wake his sleeping angel. Mike soaks up every detail, truly living in the moment because he knows it will never happen again.

He walks across the penthouse suite to the balcony, hoping that fresh air will do him some good. Looking out at the skyline of San Antonio, Mike thinks to himself, *I'm gonna miss this beautiful city.* The fresh air helps to ease the anxiety that has a grip on him. *Fuck, I need to calm down and get some sleep,* he thinks to himself. *A cold shower typically does the trick.*

Turning on the shower, Mike stands there, letting the water run down his body. The sound of the shower and the coldness of the water sends a shock to his senses and dulls them to the point he loses himself. Suddenly, he is startled by a pair of hands gripping his hips and sliding up to his chest.

She enters the shower, pulls Mike close, and holds him tight. Instantly, Mike is at peace as she hugs him and kisses the nape of his neck. "Nightmares?" she asks.

With a slight motion of his head, *"Yes,"* he replies.

She whispers, "Sorry, my love."

They stand there holding each other for what seems like an eternity. Eventually, they return to the bed, where she comforts him, allowing him to break down and fall apart until they both drift off together.

Before their final moments of consciousness, Mike whispers, "I love you, Em."

She replies, "To the moon and stars."

* * *

A few months later, Mike appears calm on the surface, but his mind is running a million miles a minute. Internally, he runs through his pre-combat checklists and pre-combat inspections. He mentally checks and rechecks his packing list, tries to recall if he put out all the information to his guys, and various other things, in preparation for the call.

"Son...son..."

Mike's thoughts snap back to his family dinner. "Yes, Papi," he replies.

Tomas asks, "Are you okay? You seem to be off in space."

"Yeah, I'm good. Just making sure I'm...we...we are ready."

"Mijo, I have the utmost confidence in you. You are an expert in your craft and are smartish at best. I know you dedicated countless hours of prepping and training for this. You and your men are ready. I know you can't promise you'll make it back, but do everything you can to come home to your wife and kids."

Mike stares at Tomas with a huge smirk. Tomas knows that grin well; it's a grin that precedes a smart-ass comment.

"Dad, what the hell? So what you're saying is you're here to see me off, but when I get back, you don't want to see me anymore? Cool. I got it. But you forget one thing—"

Interrupting, Tomas interjects, "What's that?"

"I know where you live, plus I have a key to your house. And don't think about changing the locks 'cause I know how to break into my bedroom window. Used to do it all the time and never got caught," Mike retorts.

"Well, son...two things."

"Yeah, what's that?"

"I let you think you got away with breaking into the house. When you were drunk and stoned at three in the morning, you were not quiet at all. A deaf man could hear you coming into the house. And, second, what if I move?"

Mike snaps back without missing a beat, "Well, Dad, there are only five Hispanic families in Burk. I'll just look for the house with the piñatas and a kick-ass Nova in the driveway. And if that fails, Jose will tell me where you live for five bucks."

They laugh, and María chimes in, "*Ya apacíguate.* We are at dinner. You need to behave."

Both men look at Maria and reply in unison, "Fine."

Mike's phone rings. The table instantly falls silent, and all eyes focus on the phone and Mike. They know what it means. They had expected it, but had hoped it wouldn't come.

Mike looks across to Vanessa, who is on the verge of tears. He answers the phone, "Hello… Hey, First Sergeant… Roger." Indistinguishable chatter is heard on the other side of the phone; then Mike continues, "Roger, First Sergeant. I'll make the call now. I'll follow up when complete and give you a status update. Roger, see you then." Mike hangs up the phone and looks at everyone. "Well, it was a spam call. They wanted to contact me about my car's factory warranty."

The entire table lets out a nervous laugh.

Mike takes a deep breath. "No, but seriously, we have to report at 0300 to the company. Then we will fly out sometime after that. Excuse me, though; I have to make some calls. I have an hour to make notifications and give an update."

Vanessa's and Maria's eyes begin to swell with tears. They try to keep strong for Logan, Jami, and Lexi, who softly begin to cry.

Lexi, Mike's youngest daughter, pulls at his shirt. "Daddy, I don't want you to go. I'm gonna miss you, and who is gonna keep the monsters away?"

Mike fights back his tears and tries to steady his trembling voice. "I know, princess. I will miss y'all too. I will think about you every day. As for the monsters…well, that's where Logan and Jami come in. While I'm gone, they will look after you and help fight off the monsters." Mike kisses Lexi's forehead sweetly, then gets up to do what is required of him.

* * *

Eight hours later, Mike and his family arrive at the company area. Mike finds a place to park in the parking lot across from the back deck of the company building. "It looks like some of the guys are here already," Mike tells Tomas as they see groups of soldiers and their family members clustering together.

"Mijo, were do you need us to be?"

"I'm gonna grab my stuff and find a place to ground my gear and go draw my weapon. You guys can wait in the car or hang out by my gear," answered Mike.

Mike exits the car and grabs his three olive-green duffle bags from the trunk of the car. He puts one on his back, securing it tightly. Then takes another bag and slides his arms in the arm loops, bringing it to his chest. The last bag, he grabs in his left hand, ensuring that his right hand remains free in case he has to render the proper greeting to an officer.

Mike moves purposefully toward the street with Tomas, Maria, Vanessa, and the kids a little ways behind him.

"Mike, wait a sec," called out Tomas. "Let me help you." Tomas sped up to take one of the duffle bags from Mike.

"Thanks, Papi, we don't need to go that far."

Mike and his family cross the street and claim a small piece of pavement in front of the loading dock of the company building. Mike plops his gear on the cement pavement. "This is good enough for government work," said Mike. "All right, guys, I'm gonna go check in, grab my weapon, and see if anything changed. You guys can stay right here, and I'll be back."

"Dad, I want to come with you," said Logan.

Mike kneels down to get to Logan's height and says, "Mijo, you can't right now. I need you to be my special helper and guard my gear. You need to fight off anyone that comes near it. Okay?"

Logan looks Mike dead in the eyes and says, "Even if it's Carson?"

"Especially if it is Carson. He likes to steal my socks and underwear when I am not looking."

"Okay, Dad. I will guard your stuff."

Mike leaves his family by his army gear, walks up the steps of the back dock, and disappears into the company area to draw his weapon and get any updates. Fifteen minutes pass before Mike reappears with his M4 attached to his body. As he exits the door, he sees a short, wiry soldier and his family standing next to Vanessa and the kids.

Mike could recognize Carson's five-foot-five, 135-pound frame, and North Carolina accent from a mile away. Although Carson was short in stature, he was as fierce as they come. Mike once saw Carson drag a 220-pound man one hundred meters, then effortlessly throw the man on his shoulders and run another one hundred meters to safety.

Carson and Mike have known each other the longest out of everyone in the platoon. They went to medic training together and then were stationed in the same unit at Fort Hood. They have deployed twice before with each other. Over the years, they have grown close and shared just about every life event. Carson was there when Mike was injured on his first deployment. Mike was Carson's best man at his and Jess's wedding. Mike and Carson were there for the births of each other's children.

Their wives are also very close. Jess and Vanessa check in on each other when Mike and Carson are in the field or deployed.

Logan is the first to see Mike come out of the company, and he shouts as loud as he can, "Dad, I stopped Carson from stealing your stuff by punching him in the balls."

Mike smiles while the crowd of soldiers and family members within earshot of Logan roar with laughter. "Serves him right. He knows better than to try to mess with my stuff."

Laughing, Carson turns to Mike. "Hey, man, why did you have the li'l shark guard your stuff? You know he shows no mercy."

"Cuz I told you many times to stop fucking with my shit. I finally had to make sure you get the message," Mike said, chuckling, as he walked down the steps to rejoin his family.

Mike approaches Carson and gives him a big hug. Then turns to Jess, Carson's wife, and gives her a hug and a kiss on the cheek.

"Mike, please watch out for this one. He needs to come back in one piece to take care of this little one," she said as she rocked a three-month-old baby.

Mike smiles and starts talking in a baby voice, "I'll make sure your papa comes home, little one. I promise. Uncle Mike will make sure of that."

Carson shakes his head and says, "What the fuck? I'm right here. I am not that reckless."

Vanessa interrupts, "Um, excuse me. The burnt patch of grass in my backyard says differently." Vanessa turns to Tomas and Maria. "One time, Mike and Carson tried to grill in the backyard, and the charcoal would not light. So Carson, in his infinite wisdom, decided to pour half a gallon of gasoline in the grill then light it. A huge fireball engulfed the grill and flaming drops of gasoline dripped on the ground, catching a two-foot patch of grass on fire. Logan comes running into the house, yelling, 'Mom! Dad and Carson need an adult. The house is on fire! Save them.' Me and Jess go outside and see them pouring beer and trying to stomp out the flames. Mind you, they had a perfectly good, working hose next to them. So I grabbed the hose and put out the fire. After that, we had to supervise them when grilling."

"That wasn't my fault. And I don't know why you are bringing up old shit. It's not like it didn't work. Plus, that was some of the best barbeque we've ever had," said Carson, laughing.

Mike smiles and adds, "We had the situation under control the whole time." Then he looks at Logan and asks, "Right, mijo?"

Logan shakes his head and says, "Nope. Y'all needed an adult."

Mike's jaw dropped, and he said, "Wow, mijo. How quickly you jump ship."

Logan responded, "I like living."

Maria looks at Mike and gently slaps his arm. "Mijo, you shouldn't be drinking and cooking."

Mike laughs and shakes off Maria's slap. "Ma, we only had three beers. Plus, it's not like Dad did much better."

Tomas laughs and moves out of arm's reach of Maria. "Oh no. Don't bring me into this."

"What is he talking about, Tomas?" asked Maria.

Tomas inches farther away and answers, "Nothing. He is just trying to deflect the blame." Tomas shoots Mike a look to make him shut up.

Mike acknowledges it and laughs even harder.

"Did you already check in?" asked Carson.

"Yeah, we need to get the guys formed up and draw weapons. Once we have an up on everyone being here, we are to stand fast until we move to Ironhorse Gym. From there, we will need to wait until they call our flights," answered Mike.

"Word. Aight, well, I'm gonna go draw my weapon and come back out. You mind keeping the wife and kids company?" asked Carson.

"Oh, of course, we will," answered Vanessa.

Carson jogs up the stairs and disappears into the company.

As more of the soldiers from Mike's platoon begin to arrive, he gives them instructions, takes roll call, and greets their families. Mike looks toward the parking lot and sees a behemoth of a man carrying all of his bags on his shoulders. From a distance, Mike could tell that it was Chris.

Chris stood six feet four inches tall and weighed around 240 pounds. You would never assume he was a native Texan from how he talked or dressed. This would be Chris's second deployment with Mike, but, like Carson, Chris and his wife spent most of their free time with Mike and Vanessa. Chris's wife, Crystal, was not a typical Army spouse. She was also in the Army and was assigned to Mike and Chris's medical support company.

As a joke, Mike tells two soldiers in formation to go help Chris, knowing that he will feel insulted and send them away.

From a distance, Mike hears Chris yelling at the young troopers, "What the fuck do I look like? I ain't a fucking weakling. Get the fuck outta here. Who fucking sent you?"

One of the troopers shakingly answered, "Uh, Staff Sergeant Perez."

Chris looks up and sees Mike laughing uncontrollably. Chris shakes his head and gives Mike the middle finger.

Carson walks out of the company and sees Mike laughing. "What the fuck did I miss?" he asks.

"I sent those two soldiers to help Chris with his bags, and he lit into them."

Carson starts laughing and says, "I wish I could have seen his face."

"Oh, it was fucking priceless."

"You guys are such assholes," said Vanessa.

"Yeah, why do you guys have to be like that?" chimed in Jess.

"Because it is a rite of passage. We were fucked with when we were privates, and now we are passing on the torch," said Mike.

Carson adds, "Yeah. I remember when we first came to the unit. Lucas asked us if we liked our shit pushed in."

Mike laughs. "Yeah, I forgot about that. He had just watched that movie *Training Day*. And for some reason, he thought that was the best way to welcome us to the unit."

Chris finally made it to the group and, laughing, said, "You guys are fucking assholes."

"You looked like you needed help, old man. And it just shows how good you trained your peeps. They saw you on the struggle bus and just sat there looking at you and laughing. Saying, 'Fuck that guy,'" Mike said laughingly.

"What? Those fucks. Hey, dicks, get over here!" Chris calls out.

The two soldiers came running over to Chris and stood with their arms behind their backs in the position of parade rest. "Yes, Sergeant," they said in unison.

"You guys said, 'Fuck me,' huh?" asked Chris.

The two soldiers looked at each other, both confused. "Uh, no, we didn't, Sergeant."

Vanessa turned to Mike and said, "Stop it. You are gonna get those poor boys roughed up."

Mike lets out an even louder laugh and says, "Dude, I'm just fucking with you. They didn't even see you."

Chris looks at Mike. "Mike, you play too much. You were about to get these kids killed before they even made it to combat."

Chris greets Mike and Carson again with hugs; then he turns and also gives Jess and Vanessa hugs. Mike introduces Chris to Tomas and Maria.

"Did Crystal already leave?" asked Jess.

"Yeah, she left yesterday, so it was just me and my dad at the house. He just dropped me off and had to take off back to Dallas for work tonight."

"Aw, well, at least you will catch up with her soon," said Vanessa.

"Yeah. And she talked to her command, and we might get to live together over there. So that's good, but excuse me; I need to go check in and grab my Pew Pew Stick. Do you guys mind watching my stuff?"

"Yeah, we got you, dude," answered Mike.

Chris ascends the stairs and disappears into the company to check in.

Mike looked around the company area and soaked in the sight. He noticed, as time passed, more and more soldiers arrived at the unit with their families. He could feel the pulsing energy around the company; it was a mix of excitement, fear, and sadness. For some, this was the first time that their loved ones would be in harm's way. While others had experienced this several times before.

Loud music with palpable bass beats screeches into the parking lot, breaking into Mike's thoughts. He looks around and sees a silver Dodge Magnum pull into a parking space.

Carson taps Mike and points to the Magnum. "Looks like Lucas is here."

Mike nods his head in acknowledgment and chuckles.

"Do you know who is here with Lucas?" asked Vanessa.

"Nope, I don't. I know he said he was staying the night with a friend," Mike said while making air quotes with his fingers when he said the word *friend.*

Jess shakes her head. "That man will never settle down."

The spectacle of Lucas's entrance grabs the attention of the soldiers and family members. They witness Lucas get out of the passenger's side of his car and walk to the back. A long-legged, blonde-haired, slender Latina woman gets out of the driver's side, walks to the rear of the Magnum, and meets Lucas. Lucas, who stands at five foot six and 180 pounds, looks like a toddler standing next to the woman. The woman grabs Lucas, pulls him close, and gives him the most passionate and graphicly sexy kiss she could, then walks back to the driver's side. Lucas stands there, momentarily dazed, before opening the trunk and grabbing his gear. He shuts the trunk, and the car speeds away.

"Lucas, honey, pick up your jaw. She already left," Vanessa shouts, laughing from across the street.

Lucas spots Mike and the group and walks toward them with the biggest smile Mike has ever seen.

"So that was your friend?" asked Jess, chuckling.

Lucas continues to smile and with a thick, Puerto Rican accent answers, "Yeah, her name is Stephanie, and I think I am in love."

"What about Samantha?" asked Mike.

"Or Julie?" added Carson.

"I love them too," answered Lucas.

"You are such a dog," said Jess.

Lucas starts to howl and laugh. "I'd love to stay and chat, but I know I'm late. So let me check in and grab my shit." Lucas rushes up the stairs as Chris comes out.

"Hey, Lucas, First Sergeant is looking for you," said Chris.

"I know; he called me three times already," answered Lucas as he entered the door.

A few minutes later, Lucas comes out and asks Mike, Carson, and Chris if everyone is present. They give him a thumbs-up, and he disappears into the company again.

The first sergeant comes out and gives the unit the command to fall in for roll call. He tells the platoon sergeants to ensure everyone is there and somewhat sober.

Three in the morning comes and goes, and at eight in the morning, the entire company makes their way to the Ironhorse Gym, where they do what the Army does best—hurry up and wait. Finally, twelve p.m. comes, and Mike's flight number is called.

He calls out to his men, "Platoon...Atten-TION," and in unison, they snap to attention and file out of the musty gymnasium in which they'd just spent the last five hours waiting. He notices some of his men crying as they leave the gym, an expected reaction given the task they are being asked to accomplish.

Mike is the last to go, and as he exits the gym, he sees why his men are crying. There stands his Logan in the doorway, saluting everyone who exited the gym. For an hour straight, he held his salute, never faltering, never wavering. Some of Mike's soldiers couldn't even do that if asked. Mike bears witness to this sight and breaks down sobbing. He can no longer fight back his own emotions.

Mike returns his son's salute, drops to his knees, and gives Logan a big hug. Then he stands and makes his way to the bus that is taking him to his plane. The bus leaves the gym parking lot and heads to the airfield ten minutes away.

Sitting on the bus, Mike stares out the window. His mind is already in the distant land he visited a few times before. Reliving the horrors he witnessed, participated in, and encountered.

"Sarge, are you ready?" Big Country asks. "Sarge, are you ready to kill some haji and deliver freedom to dem Iraqis?"

Mike returns to the present as Big Country repeats his question. "Country, I appreciate your enthusiasm, but that mission is over. We are there to train their army, keep the peace, and"—using air quotes—"win the hearts and minds of the Iraqi people."

"Nah, Sarge, that's not why I joined."

"Well, Country, I'll meet you halfway. Let's say I pray for peace, but I'm ready for war," replied Mike.

"Shit yeah, Sarge, I'll take that."

Arriving at the terminal, a huge smile appears on Mike's face because he knows in a few minutes he will see the second most important woman on this trip. She is simply known as the Soldier's Last Embrace. He eagerly gets in line to get his fifth hug from her. Her gentle face and warm smile give Mike a sense of peace and assurance that this deployment will be better than his last two.

Mike roams the airport terminal, checking on his men. His newer soldiers pick Mike's brain on how he thinks this deployment will turn out. The soldiers he previously deployed with talk about the experiences from their earlier deployments and recount the good times. Mike shudders at the thought that those times were considered good.

Stopping to think about it, a better definition would be the word *simple*. Those times were simple. You had a clear mission, you had a clear enemy, and you did not have all the inconsequential things involved in everyday life.

Over the intercom, a voice announces, "Chalk Leaders for flight 773, flight 774, and flight 779, report to the check-in desk. Chalk Leaders for flight 773, flight 774, and flight 779, report to the check-in desk."

Carson, Lucas, and Chris, Mike's most trusted friends and confidants, shout from across the crowded terminal, "Hey, dick, get your head out of your ass. We need to check in."

Mike breaks from his thoughts and joins his friends. He knows the time is near and that soon he and his men will be wheels up and making their way to their new home for a year.

Carson asks, "You guys ready?" After Mike and the others nod in agreement, Carson states, "Let's just hope that this peacekeeping mission is not like our last." They all chuckle and smile.

Their first deployment together was supposed to be a peacekeeping mission—well, at least that was what they were told. While doing their handoff with the unit they were replacing, they were told that they hadn't seen an ounce of combat, never had to fire their weapons or detain anyone. Then, one week after the transition took effect, the events of Bloody Sunday occurred. Bloody Sunday completely altered their mission as peacekeepers.

Mike, Carson, Lucas, and Chris make their way to the check-in desk to receive their next set of instructions, gather their troops, and board the plane. Mike overhears flight-attendant jokes, jokes about joining the mile-high club, and questions about this flight serving alcohol. They all knew that it doesn't, but it didn't hurt to ask. Mike completes his final checks and reports to his higher command that all the sensitive items and personnel are present and accounted for.

As the flight attendants seal the plane and conduct their inspections, overhead, the pilot announces, "Hey, boys.

You make this land proud. Keep your heads on a swivel, stay alert…"

The entire plane shouts back, "Stay alive!"

The overwhelming sound of 150 trained and eager killers sends a swell of emotion through Mike.

The pilot continues, "Y'all look out for each other, and come back home in one piece. OORAH!"

The entire plane responds, "HOOAH!"

Mike laughs and looks at Carson. "Well, fuck, we have a jarhead flying the plane. Now we don't have to worry about dying in combat if we never make it there."

Carson shakes his head. "Don't worry," he says as he pulls out a small pack of crayons his daughter gave him before he left, "I got a snack for him in case he gets hungry and his blood sugar gets low." They both laugh. "Well, Mike, it's time for our tradition," Carson says as he pulls out a nip small enough for one shot.

Mike reaches into his pocket and pulls out his.

Carson starts, "To hell and back…"

Mike continues the toast, "Always moving forward, never moving back."

They chug their nips and get ready for takeoff. Mike closes his eyes as he puts on his headphones, through which he hears a playlist of songs that remind him of a distant memory. He could not escape a nagging thought, *This time...this time, it is going to be different.*

Chapter 2

"Doc...Doc..."

Mike is startled awake and, in his semiconscious state, sees Em's face. He focuses on her face and slowly looks around the room, trying to remember where he is. His heart begins to race as fear starts to set in.

Em gently comforts him and takes his hand into hers. "Mike, it's time for you to wake up."

Mike replies, "No, I don't want to."

A loud and thunderous knock snaps Mike awake from his blissful escape. The knocks get louder and are coupled with, "Doc... Doc...wake up."

Mike slowly stumbles out of bed and makes his way to the door. As he gains his bearings, he recognizes that the deep voice coming from the other side of the door belongs to Jonny Esparza.

Jonny, more colloquially known as the Sasquatch, had been with Mike on all of his deployments. On his first deployment, he was dubbed the Sasquatch because of his uncanny ability to move swiftly, despite his large frame. Standing at six four and coming in at just under 260 pounds, he could outrun most of the gazelles in the unit. Additionally, Jonny was covered from neck to feet in an ungodly amount of body hair.

The shouting intensifies, "C'MON, DOC, GET YOUR ASS UP. WE GOTTA GO."

Mike opens the door, responding, "What the fuck do you want, man? We are supposed to be down right now."

"I know, Doc, but shit popped off at the Alamo. Our replacements are getting slaughtered right now."

Mike retorts, "So. That sounds like a *them* problem."

Sasquatch replies, "Yeah, typically I would agree, but Demon Company went to assist, and now they have three platoons separated and pinned down. They took some casualties and have some catastrophic kills on three vics."

"Fuck!" Mike could feel his heart racing and breathing quickening. Up until these last two months, this deployment seemed relatively calm when compared to his last two. But with the recent increase in enemy attacks, Mike had a feeling that it was only a matter of time before shit really hit the fan. It looked as if it just did.

"C'mon, Doc. We gotta be at the TOC in ten minutes."

"'Kay," Mike replies, "I'll be there." Mike shuts the door and quickly gets dressed, grabs his go bag and snacks, because he knows how these missions turn out. He plans not to be back to his hut for at least a few days.

Mike does one final check to make sure he has everything he needs, turns off the lights, and blows a kiss to a picture of his family taped to the wall. They are the last things he sees when he leaves and the first things he looks at when he returns to his hut.

Mike trots to the motor pool where the Tactical Operations Center is co-located. As he makes his way, he notices Carson in a dead sprint heading to the Bandog Tactical Operations Center. Mike yells out, "What the fuck you doing?"

Carson manages to reply, "MASCAL. Tarmiyah attacked!" As Carson manages to squeeze out his last statement, as loud explosion rings out in the distance, from the direction of Tarmiyah. Mike and Carson stop dead in their tracks, and their jaws drop as they witness the enormous black-and-gray mushroom-cloud plume of smoke propel into the air.

After seeing the explosion off in the distance, Mike and Carson take off in a dead sprint to the TOC. They know that Chris is out in Tarmiyah with a few of the younger guys from the Medic Platoon, along with their combat element.

Mike estimates, from the size of the smoke plume, the distance he was from Tarmiyah, and the time it took from seeing the explosion to hearing the sound, the bomb had to have been over 500 pounds of explosives. Mike thinks of all the possible injuries, enemy-attack plans, evacuation plans, and supplies that the guys might need in case their aid station was destroyed.

His thoughts race as he fears the worst for Chris. Mike tries to hope for the best and think good thoughts. Deep down, however, he knows the odds that Chris survived a blast like that are very low. Very, very low.

Mike finally makes it to the TOC, and upon entering, he hears radio chatter from the stranded elements under attack.

"Demon Mike, this is Red One; we are under attack. Estimated enemies' counts are at least sixty. Complex attack of small arms, RPGs, and one VBIED. The attack was coordinated. Currently four KIA, fifteen wounded, three unaccounted for. Request air and ground support. Additional request for medical support and ammo. Currently red on ammo. I repeat, we are red on ammo."

Mike's heart stops. From first reports, the attack sounds worse than he originally suspected.

Captain O'Neill and the last platoon leader arrive from the battalion TOC and begin to issue the operational plan to aid the company under attack. Each platoon acknowledges their role and begins moving to their waiting seventy-two-ton steeds of pure destruction.

"Doc," Captain O'Neill starts, "you ready?"

Mike replies, "Sir, let's do this! We are wasting time talking, and we both have skin in this game." Mike knew that Captain O'Neill's best friend, Captain Baker, was commanding the company that was under attack.

With one last order, Captain O'Neill tells his combat element, "Load up, and we will do a rolling-ramp brief."

Mike and Captain O'Neill hurry to their tanks, where the rest of the crew was loaded up and ready to go. Mike jumps down into the loader's hatch and slips on his armored communication helmet and Kevlar vest.

"Sir," Mike shouts, "anything I need to know before we get there?"

Captain O'Neill holds up two fingers, prompting Mike to switch to comms channel two. Then he replies, "Doc, first reports do not look good. The whole damn city is trying to kill the boys of Demon Company. Guidance from higher is to take care of business and get our boys home safe."

Mike replies, "Got it." He switches his comms back to the normal frequencies so he can assist Captain O'Neill in coordinating the battle.

Captain O'Neill transmits over the radio, "Cobra TOC. Cobra Six. Four vics, fourteen PAX. SP time now with all sensitive items accounted for. How copy? Over."

A reply comes across the radio, "Cobra Six, Cobra TOC. That's a good copy. Give 'em hell, sir. Over."

Captain O'Neill replies, "Roger." He then calls out across the internal comms of the tank, "Guys, stay alert. There is no telling what we are rolling up to."

Sergeant Marks answers in his thick Filipino accent, "Sir, while you switched channels, Long Knife One came on the net. They've currently seen as many as 120 hajis closing in on Demon Company. They engaged with hellfire missles and guns, and created some breathing room for the boys of Demon Company. They also said that they see three convoys of enemy troops heading toward Tarmiyah for reinforcements."

Mike thinks to himself, *Son of a bitch. These fuckers came to play.*

On the surface, Mike looked calm and focused on the mission he and his team were about to encounter. However, deep-down feelings of hate and anger began boiling up within him. He knew these feelings all too well, especially after his first deployment and the events surrounding Bloody Sunday. These feelings scared and excited him. His hands and his knees slightly trembled from the surge of adrenaline swelling in his body.

Mike stood at belly-button defilade in the loader's hatch, with one hand on the grip of the loader's M240 machine gun, and carefully scanned his sector of fire. Mike briefly closed his eyes and steadied his breathing, trying to regain his center, which was very difficult with heavy-metal music blaring on the tank's internal comms.

Captain O'Neill and Mike were still about ten minutes out, just making the turn at checkpoint 59A, when White One came across the company net, "Cobra Six, White One." The familiar sound of the coax's firing rang in the background of the radio transmission. Mike could also hear the fire command echo across the radio net.

"Go ahead, White One," Captain O'Neill replied just before a loud and thunderous boom echoed off in the distance.

Mike smiled and felt his dick get a little hard from recognizing the sound of the fire-breathing dragon letting loose on the world its 120 mm cannon of death and destruction.

Sergeant Marks, jumping up and down in his gunner seat, with excitement chimed over the internal comms, "Fuck yeah!! We about to have some fun today."

White One continued, "We are first on scene, break. Engaging with large amounts of small arms and RPGs, break. Estimated enemy count is seventy, eighty armed fighters. Over."

Captain O'Neill responded, "Good copy. Blue Platoon should be three mikes out, followed by Red Platoon, break. When they arrive, you push to the south. Blue Platoon will push past the water plant to the east and cut off reinforcements. Red Platoon and the Headquarters element will run a wedge formation into the heart of the city and help secure the LZ. How copy? Over."

Over the radio came the responses from the platoons, "White One. Roger."

"Blue One, acknowledged."

"Red One, loud and clear."

Switching back to internal comms, Captain O'Neill informed Mike and the others, "All right, guys, once we wedge in and secure a footprint, Doc, you dismount, link up with the medics from Demon Company, and start working the evac plan."

Mike responded, "Gotcha, sir."

Captain O'Neill gives the command to go closed-hatch as rounds begin to ricochet off the top of the tank. The sounds of enemy rounds are drowned out as Sergeant Marks opens fire with the coax gun. The clanking of hot, expended brass silences the deafening sound of the tank's engine.

Mike tries to monitor the situation on the ground over the radios, while Captain O'Neill and Sergeant Marks call out targets and possible enemy-fire positions.

"Doc! Doc," Sergeant Marks cries out, "get ready to load a can round."

Mike's muscle memory takes over, and before he realizes it, a canister round is loaded in the breach of the 120 mm main gun. The breach door is sliding up, and Mike is bracing himself against the hull of the tank turret.

Grabbing the main safety, Mike shouts over the comms, "UP!"

In a fraction of a second, the turret fills with the smell of gunpowder, and a cloud of dust obscures vision inside the tank.

Sergeant Marks screams, "Doc, another!"

Mike repeats the process without any hesitation. "UP!" he yells.

BOOM!

There's a gut-punching reverberation from the resultant change in pressure when the fire-breathing dragon is unleashed.

Ten minutes pass, but ten minutes in the middle of a firefight feels like a lifetime. Finally, Captain O'Neill believes there was a strong enough foothold on the city. He calls out to Mike, "Doc, I think we are good for now. Link up with the medics from Demon Company, and start coordinating the evac plan. Demon Red is sending out a small team to take you to where the rest are holing up."

Mike nods as he switches his helmets, grabs his gear, and dismounts from the tank, linking up with an element of Demon Red Platoon. Mike and the members of Demon Red conduct three- to five-second rushes, using the debris and scattered rubble littered throughout the city as cover to block any bullets that are looking for them. Mike scans his surroundings and sees sections missing from the Demon compound as a result of the blast.

Mike finally makes it to a two-story house and enters through the front door. He is taken back upon entering because although the front of the house is intact, except for a few bullet holes, the inside reveals the true extent of the damage caused by the explosion. On the first-floor east-facing wall, the corner of the house is missing after taking a hit from two RPGs. The second story of the east-facing wall has several large holes from both the initial explosion and RPG fire.

On the south-facing wall, a medium-sized hole in the center of the dining room served as a quick exfil route if the soldiers from Demon Company had to quickly abandon the house dubbed the Alamo.

Staff Sergeant St. Clare shouts out to Mike, "Boy, Doc Chris is gonna be glad to see you."

The right corner of Mike's mouth curls up as he responds, "I bet he is. He always calls me to unfuck his fuckups."

Staff Sergeant St. Clare chuckles slightly in a fleeting moment of relief after the chaos he and his team just endured.

"Chris," Mike calls out as he lays eyes on his brother; his heart skips a few beats, coupled with a wrenching gut punch. Mike quickly did a visual assessment of Chris and his injuries. Overall, Chris could not be too badly injured since he was hobbling around, providing care to his team, and directing the other medics who were with him.

Chris looks at Mike and states, "Hey, dick, glad to see you finally made it, now that I did all the heavy lifting."

Mike shakes his head and responds, "Well, fuck-face, it's about time you do some fucking work. All you've done this tour is eat, sleep, and get yoked."

They both share a quick laugh, and at that moment, they reassure one another that everything will be all right. Mike shifts his focus to the task at hand. "So what we got," he asks.

Chris responds, "Aight, so we got fifteen wounded. Three litter-bound. Of those three, two have lower-extremity wounds. Tourniquets were placed at 1015, and the last reassess was five mikes ago. Still stable, I have them pulling security on the door. The third has second- and third-degree burns on about sixty-five percent of his body." Chris lowers his voice, "Bro, all I'm doing with him is trying to keep him calm and comfortable. It's a toss-up if he makes it. The remaining twelve are all walking wounded, mostly suffering shrapnel wounds and a few gunshot wounds to the extremities."

Mike asks, "What about you?"

"I'm good, man. A few bumps and bruises, but nothing I can't handle. I was outside on the back corner of the compound, making rounds on the guys when the VBIED went off."

Mike shakes his head in disbelief and states, "You lucky fuck. Where's the mic? Let's confirm that it's calmed down enough to get this evac going."

Chris points over to a handheld radio in the center of the room of litter-bound soldiers.

Mike changes the radio frequency to communicate with Captain O'Neill. "Cobra Six, Snake Charmer Seven. Over."

Captain O'Neill responds, "Goddammit, Doc, that's not your call sign."

Mike smirks. "Fine. Cobra Six, Cobra Lifeline. Over."

Captain O'Neill answers, "Cobra Lifeline, Cobra Six."

"What's the SITREP outside? We good to start our evac? Over."

Captain O'Neill transmits, "Cobra Lifeline, Cobra Six. Roger. We have secured the city and have established a secure defensive position around the LZ. Our Green and Gold elements have entered the city and are staged to assist with CASEVAC of the walking wounded. Over."

Mike states, "Cobra Six, Cobra Lifeline. Good copy. Sending up the nine line now, and I will make my exfil with our Gold element. Over."

"Cobra Lifeline, good copy. Over. Cobra Six. Out."

Mike switches over to the MEDEVAC frequency and calls up his report to have the medical helicopters come and pick up the litter-bound soldiers. Within ten minutes, the helicopters are touching down inside the makeshift helicopter-landing zone in a nearby soccer field. Five minutes after that, the three soldiers are loaded onto the bird and off to the Green Zone for medical care.

Mike walks with Chris to the back of a Bradley Fighting Vehicle and makes sure he is good. He looks at Chris sitting on the bench inside the Bradley and says, "Aight there, little buddy. I have you all tucked in. Daddy scared off the bad guys for you. So don't be scared."

Chris cracks a smile through his dust- and blood-covered face and laughs loudly. He responds, "You're such a fucking asshole. I might just buy you a beer when we get back...maybe."

Mike steps back and watches the ramp of the Bradley rise and lock, then makes his way to the Gold Four Humvee and loads up to return to base. He buckles in behind Sergeant First Class Miller in the back of the truck.

Sergeant First Class Miller turns, looks at Mike, and asks, "You ready, Doc?"

After Mike nods, the sergeant grabs the mic and broadcasts over the radio, "All elements, this is Gold Four. SP time now. Let's get the fuck outta this hellhole."

The various combat elements respond and begin their movement back to Camp Taji. In the front of the convoy are four tanks from Red Platoon, followed by two Bradleys from Green Platoon. Then came the Head-quarters Platoon, followed by two gun trucks from Gold Platoon, and the convoy was closed out by the four tanks from White Platoon.

Remaining at the Alamo was Blue Platoon, two Brad-leys from Green Platoon with twenty dismounted infantry soldiers, and four gun trucks from Gold Platoon with twelve dismounted infantry soldiers.

Captain O'Neill thought it was best to maintain a small force to keep a presence in the city. They would remain in place until the replacement unit could regroup and send additional teams to secure the city. The remaining troops would also serve as a quick-reaction force in the event the insurgents tried to return and attack the city.

Chapter 3

Mike was sitting in the back of the truck, looking out the window. His body ached, and he felt drained. Inhaling deeply and letting out a big sigh, Mike tried to remember the last time he took a moment to breathe. The wave of adrenaline he felt heading to Tarmiyah was receding, and all he felt was exhaustion.

Staring off into the distance, Mike's mind traveled into the future as he thought about the unit's homecoming a few months away. The thought of being home and seeing Vanessa and the kids brought a smile to his face. The moment of happiness quickly passed as he remembered that the happiness of returning home would be short-lived.

Mike reflected on the email he received from Em a few weeks ago. Em, his sweet Em. Mike could not imagine the pain and trouble he caused her…and the bomb he was about to deliver to Vanessa and the kids.

Mike continues to stare out the window, letting his mind wander for what seems like an eternity. He comes back to the present when he notices off in the distance a small glint of light. A few minutes pass, and then he notices another…then another…and another. Mike scans and analyzes his surroundings, suddenly realizing where the convoy is.

Mike yells out, "Stop the fucking truck."

Sergeant First Class Miller turns around with a look of bewilderment at the same time that the driver stomps on the gas. Sergeant First Class Miller manages to get out, "The fuck—" before a loud and thunderous boom rips through the cab of the Humvee.

Mike sees a fireball of red, orange, and pink flames come hurling toward his head—

* * *

Nothing but darkness…

Mike attempts to speak, but cannot utter any words. He struggles to breathe. His ears ring, and his head pounds from the blast. He is dazed and slightly confused, and his back feels like a million needles are being stabbed into it.

After what seems like a few minutes, his sight returns, and he sees Specialist Clark, the driver, slumped over the steering wheel. Sergeant First Class Miller is grabbing his helmet and reaching for Specialist Clark.

Specialist Clark begins to move, so Mike feels better. *At least Clark is not dead,* he thought.

Mike can hear the radio chatter from the rest of the convoy. From what he can gather, the bomb detonated in the rear of the truck. The gunner, Sergeant Ramon, is alive, but the back of his legs are covered in shrapnel from the blast.

Evidently, the insurgent forces were not done with the attack on Tarmiyah. They planned another coordinated attack on the convoy. Mike began to hear gunfire from enemy AK-47s and RPGs. He also heard the tanks' main and coax machine guns, the Bradleys' 25 mm cannon and coax machine gun, and the gun trucks' .50 caliber machine guns off in the distance.

As Mike began to come to his senses, he saw a Bradley pull up beside the truck and start to drop its ramp. All he could think was, *Goddammit, I hope this isn't the Bradley with Chris in it.*

As the ramp hits the ground, out of the dark belly of the armored beast, Mike sees Chris's smiling face. "'Ey, dick face, get in. What's this you said about killing all the bad guys?" Chris shouts.

Mike gives Chris the middle finger and starts helping Sergeant First Class Miller, Specialist Clark, and Sergeant Ramon get into the Bradley. He then jogs to load up as well, but is interrupted by a familiar whistle. Mike turns around and sees Chris's smile turn to a look of fear.

Chris yells out, "Mike! Get down!"

Mike drops to the ground and instinctively covers his head and face. He feels the heat from another blast on the right side of his body. Instantly, he is in excruciating pain caused by thousands of pieces of metal tearing into his flesh. He begins to fade in and out of consciousness. He closes his eyes; everything goes dark.

Off in the distance, he hears Chris's voice. "Not today. You ain't dying on me today."

Mike opens his eyes and sees Chris hovering over him, frantically working on him. A cold feeling sets in… then darkness again…

A shooting pain in his chest…then silence…

An eternity passes…

Finally, breaking the silence, Mike hears from far away, "Mike…Mike…Mike, my love. Come to me. Come to me."

Chapter 4

The sound of medical equipment beeps in the background. Mike lies in the center of the hospital room, a breathing tube and several lines connected to him giving him medications, nutrients, and other necessary things to keep him alive.

A heartbroken Vanessa sits in the corner of the hospital room, lovingly watching over Mike. A million thoughts race through her mind. *Goddammit, Mike, why did you have to go again? I told you not to be a damn hero. I don't know what I would do without you.*

A nurse enters the room, breaking Vanessa from her downward-spiraling thoughts.

"Mrs. Perez, can I get you anything?"

Vanessa wipes the tears gently from her face and answers, "No, ma'am. I am good for now. I think I'm gonna stay for a little bit longer before I call it a night and go home."

After her response, Vanessa notices that the body language of the nurse has drastically changed. She asks, "Is that okay? Can I stay a little bit longer? If it breaks the visiting policy, I can leave."

The nurse responds, "Um...no, it is not against the policy. You can stay as long as you like." Then she politely smiles and exits the room.

Vanessa thought to herself that the interaction with the nurse seemed a little odd, but quickly dismissed it. She shifted her focus back to the injured Mike in the hospital bed. Picking up where she left off, thoughts spiral in her head.

What seems like an eternity has passed when Vanessa notices a woman approaching Mike's room. The woman stops in front of the room, but does not enter when she sees Vanessa sitting in the corner. Vanessa locks eyes with the woman, and at the speed of light, it dawns on Vanessa why the nurse seemed uncomfortable with her staying later than usual.

Vanessa could see the look of concern this woman had for Mike, her Mike. Vanessa could feel a knot form in the pit of her stomach. Her second-worst fear is now front and center and staring her in the face. A swarm of emotions swells inside her. She begins to tear up and feels her face turn beet red from anger and pain.

She thinks to herself, *How can Mike do this to me? How can he do this to our family? What about our kids?* Vanessa wants to scream at the top of her lungs, she wants to run, she wants to hide, but she sits in her chair, trying to regain her composure, and waits. She fixates on the door and waits for the woman to enter the room.

Em freezes in place outside Mike's door. As she locks eyes with Vanessa, her heart stops, and she thinks to herself, *Oh no, this is not how this was supposed to go.* She breaks eye contact with Vanessa and looks at Mike. Her breath quickens, and she feels her knees turning to Jell-O. Turning her attention back to Vanessa, Em feels her stomach flipping over, and her pulse races.

She knew this day would come, but she did not want it to be like this. Mike and her discussed how he was going to tell Vanessa. She knew Mike was going to own up to his actions because, at heart, he was a good man—flawed, but a kind soul.

Taking a deep breath, Em grasps the handle of the hospital room's door and enters. As the door closes behind Em, she began to hear the nurses' station come alive in anticipation of the spectacle that was about to transpire.

Em looks at Vanessa and slowly begins in a soft and shaky voice, "Vanessa, I'm—"

She was quickly interrupted by Vanessa stating, "No. No. No. How do you know me? If you know my name, then that means you know who I am? And if you knew who I am, then how could you do what you did with Mike? *My* Mike."

Em lowers her gaze toward the floor and fights back the tears she feels surfacing.

Vanessa sees Em's tears and thinks to herself, *This woman must love him to have this much of a visceral emotional response. That must mean this is more than a one-time fling.* That epiphany infuriates Vanessa.

"Look at me," Vanessa starts with tears in her eyes and a trembling voice. "Whatever you two had, it didn't mean anything. You have *some* nerve showing up here. You were a fling; you meant nothing to him. What makes you think that he would want you here? He doesn't love you. He didn't call you every day just to hear your voice. He didn't tell you that you are his world and that *you* are the center of his world and that his whole world revolves around you. Did he? Did he? I didn't think so."

Em feels anger beginning to swell from deep within. She begins to speak; she starts to tell Vanessa everything she doesn't know about Mike and Em. She utters,

"Vanessa, I cannot imagine the pain you feel right now. You're right; I was not there through those hard times, and I am not trying to replace you—"

Vanessa interrupts, "Then why the hell are you here? Why would you show your face here?"

"I need Mike to know…" Em begins, then pauses.

"You need Mike to know what?" Vanessa's voice intensifies. "*What* do you need him to know?"

Em looks at Mike; her heart flutters, and she notices her hands trembling. She balls her hands into fists to stop them from shaking. "I just need him to know that I know what he did and that I tried," Em states.

Her vague answer sends Vanessa into a fit of rage. She yells, "You need to fucking leave right now. If I were you, I would not show my face here again. Mike is not your husband, and I suggest you never see him again."

Em looks at the floor and thinks to herself, *I know I should stay away.* But her love for Mike and the promise she made to him would not allow her to respect Vanessa's wishes. *Oh, Mike, why did you have to put me in this predicament? I know you want to be the one to tell Vanessa, but this is where we are now. You are in a coma, and I am doing my best to make good on my promise.*

"Vanessa, I…" Em pauses and thinks of how to frame her response. "I am not going to stop checking on Mike. Despite what you think, I care about him, and I owe it to him to be here. So, like it or not, I *will* still come here. You can accept that or not, but it is going to happen. You and I both know Mike. You know how he does his best to stick to his word and is loyal to a fault."

Vanessa's face reddens at the thought of Em still coming to see Mike. She takes a deep breath and says, "I can't control what happens when I am not here, but if I see you here again, it will be a bad day for you."

Em looks at Vanessa and silently nods her head in acknowledgment. Then she turns around and quietly exits the hospital room.

Chapter 5

Mike stares out the window at the passing scenery of what will be his new living location, loud gangsta rap blaring in his headphones. He dares not call it home; can't remember the last time he had one of those. Every few years, it's a different base, a different country, a different culture, but never a different situation. Mike was always the new kid in school. He always had to prove himself to the local kids. The ones who had grown up with each other since the start of their schooling.

Mike thinks to himself, *I hope this place is not like the last one. I hope that this time it will be different and that I will not have to prove myself to anybody.* He wishes to be left alone, to just make it through his last two years of high school. Mike plans to graduate, then leave home, go to college, and start his new life. A life far away from the military. A life that is only his and what he makes of it.

"Mike! Mike!" Tomas calls out, battling the music blasting out of the headphones.

Jose, Mike's younger brother, reaches across the back seat and slaps Mike on the shoulder.

Mike snaps off his headphones and shoots a piercing look at Jose. Mike's fist is clenched, his knuckles white; he's ready to punch Jose in the chest.

Jose quickly shouts, "Dad was calling you," as he brings his hands up to cover his chest.

Mike unclenches his fist and answers Tomas, "Yeah, Dad. What's up?"

"Yeah? Is that how you answer someone?" Tomas asks.

"Yes, sir? How may I be at your service?" Mike sarcastically responds, rolling his eyes.

Tomas looks at Mike in the rearview mirror. "Boy, you better watch that attitude. Look over there." Tomas points to a large, sprawling brick building. "That's your new high school. Do me a favor; don't get into trouble here. You do not have anyone in this school's office that will cover for you."

Mike looks at his new high school and mutters under his breath, "Those assholes had it coming."

"What did you say, son?"

"I said that I didn't start a single one of those fights."

Tomas chuckles. "You may not have thrown the first punch, but you knew what to say to provoke them."

Mike replies, "Well, now you're getting into semantics."

They both laugh and get yelled at by Maria, who interjects, "Mijo, please promise me you will behave here. We just drove by the church, and this Sunday I will light four candles for you."

Mike shakes his head while saying, "Okay, Mom."

Jose turns to Mike and whispers, "Yeah, you better behave, you troublemaker."

Mike whispers with a devilish smile, "Mind your business, or I'll slap the shit outta you."

Mike puts his headphones back on; this time, heavy metal is playing over the headphones. Mike closes his eyes and drifts away to the music. He thinks to himself, *I just gotta make it through the next two years. Just two years and then I can get on with my life. I can do two years. I just have to keep my head down and mouth shut, and then I'm out.* Mike softly chuckles. *It's the mouth shut that's gonna be the problem,* he thinks as he gently falls asleep.

* * *

The last week of summer arrives, and Mike and Tomas attend the newcomers' assembly in the cafeteria of Mike's new high school.

"Dad, do I really have to be here? I'm gonna figure all this shit out next week when I come here for class," Mike states.

"Watch your mouth, boy, and we are here so we can get the rules and other important information. Plus, you never know; you might meet a cute girl and make a friend."

"Dad, that is the last thing I wa—" Mike stops midsentence as, from across the cafeteria, he lays eyes on a girl dressed in an orange-and-black cheerleading outfit. Her flowing, jet-black hair and dark-caramel skin captivate Mike.

The girl catches Mike's starstruck gaze and smiles shyly as she coyly waves to Mike.

Tomas follows Mike's gaze and calls out, "Mike, Mike, I see that you are making a friend."

"No, I was trying to read that sign over there."

Tomas chuckles. "Whatever, mijo. You can't lie to your old man."

Mike lost sight of the cheerleader and looked feverishly around the cafeteria for her. He turned his head toward the glass cafeteria doors, and there, standing in front of him, was the angel he'd previously spotted.

"Hi, I'm Emily, but my friends call me Milly. You must be new here," Em said as she stuck out her hand.

Mike could feel his heart race as he struggled to breathe. He gently took Em's hand and shook it. All he could think about was how sweaty and clammy his hands were. "Uh...um...I'm Mike," he managed to squeeze out.

Em giggled softly and smiled. "So...do you play any sports, Uh...Um...Mike?" Em asked, gently teasing him.

"I wrestle and fight," Mike answered as he thought to himself, *Get it together.*

"Oh. Well, we don't have those sports here. But maybe I'll see you at the games or around school. I'm in all AP classes this year. What classes are you taking?"

Mike thinks to himself, *Wow, brains* and *beauty.* "Uh"—Mike rubs the back of his head, thinking of what to say—"I'm not sure. I think I'm just taking whatever they give me." Mike knew very well that he had all AP honor classes, but did not want to say so, out of fear of sounding like a geek.

"Well, I have to get back to the stage to do the closeout cheer. But it was nice meeting you, Um...Uh...Mike." Em lets out a small, flirtatious giggle. "I hope to see you around this year."

"Yeah, maybe I'll see you around too, Em."

Em looks back at Mike and says, "No one ever calls me that."

"Well, I do cuz I'm not like everyone else."

"I see that. I guess I'll let you." She smiled, batted her eyes at Mike, then turned and walked away.

* * *

A few months later, Mike settled in at his new school. He found himself getting along with the emo kids, even though Mike had the lower part of his head shaved, his long, jet-black hair on top had purple streaks, and he wore mostly all black. Mike did not really consider himself an emo kid. He mostly hung out with them because, like him, they felt as if they were societal outcasts. Plus, they always had the best weed in school.

It was late Friday night, and the town was all gathered for the Homecoming football game. Mike and his newfound friends were huddled under the bleachers, sharing a few joints between them. Mike did not really care much about the game. All he really cared about was being in the best place to see her—Em. From where he stood, the stadium lights shone behind her and gave her a heavenly glow. She looked like an angel on earth, a goddess sent from the heavens.

The final whistle blew, and the game was over. Mike did not know or care who won. He took one last hit from the joint as he got ready to leave; he then said his good-byes to his friends and made his way out of the stadium after the crowd died down.

Walking down the street alone, his headphones on and listening to loud rock music, drowning out the world, Mike was lost in his thoughts. He slowly strolled down the sidewalk, staring out into the empty street as the cold fall air briskly blew over his face.

Suddenly, Mike felt a hard, round object at the small of his back, and he heard a voice say, "Um... Uh...Mike, hand over your wallet and that CD player."

Mike thought, *Fuck, how am I gonna get robbed in this shitkicker town?* Any other time, Mike would have had the awareness to keep himself out of a situation like this, and the training to defend himself against an attacker. But in his altered state, he knew there was nothing he really could do.

Slowly and deliberately, Mike reached for his back pocket and said, "Look, dude. I don't want any trouble. Okay? I have ten bucks in my pocket and half a joint. You can have both."

The unknown assailant stifled a giggle and managed to utter, "Good. That's all I'm looking for."

Mike's face went from shock to his usual cocky smirk. "Em, is that you?"

Em belts a lighthearted laugh as Mike turns around. "Oh my God! You should have seen your face. One word. Priceless," she declares.

"Dammit, Em! You know I could have hurt you, right?"

"I saw you staring at me while you were toking up under the bleachers. You couldn't do a thing if you wanted to. Besides, your music was playing so loud tanks could have driven by you, and you would have never noticed," Em retorted and smiled.

Mike laughed and asked, "What are you doing walking? I thought you would be with Ronnie, celebrating the win."

"Um, first off, we lost. And second, he and the boys are going to the old grain mill to drink and do stupid guy things," Em stated. "Gosh, you really don't like football, do you?"

"Nope, I think it's a dumb game. A bunch of dudes running around, slapping each other on their butts, trying to get on top of each other. I'll pass," Mike proclaimed.

"Didn't you used to wrestle? Isn't that just two dudes in spandex trying to mount one another?"

Mike was dumbfounded and replied, "You got me there."

"So, since we are both walking, do you want to walk together?"

Mike quickly answered, "Yeah, of course," as he told himself, *Play it cool, man. Play it cool.*

They walked together, talking about their lives up until then, their favorite colors, family lives, and various other getting-to-know-you, conversational topics.

Then Em asked, "So, Mike...if you had to be any real animal in your next life, what would it be and why?"

Mike answered without a moment's delay, "A raccoon."

Em stopped dead in her tracks and asked, "A what?!"

"A raccoon."

"Why?" Em further interrogated Mike as her intrigue had been piqued.

"Well, they look like a bandit; they are highly intelligent; they can be alone or in a pack. Raccoons are very mischievous, you can wrestle them, and they like shiny objects. Now, drumroll, please…"

Em begins making a drumroll sound with her mouth and pats her thighs in a matching rhythm.

Mike continued, "The number one reason raccoons are my spirit animal is"—Mike gasped as he took a dramatic pause—"raccoons don't know how to let shit go. I mirror every one of those qualities."

Em laughed so hard she snorted between the words when she said, "You…win."

Mike was awestruck by Em's laugh and asked, "What's yours?"

Em, struggling to catch her breath, managed to answer, "A lion. But after hearing your explanation, I think I might want to be a raccoon too. Hey, maybe we could be a pack?"

Mike answered, "Only if you promise to never let me go."

Em stopped, stared into Mike's big brown eyes, and said, "Mike, I don't know why, but I feel like I could never let you go. Something deep down is telling me, somehow, I know our fates will be forever tied together. I never make promises I don't intend on keeping."

Mike lost himself in Em's eyes. Deep down, he knew Em would stand by her promise. His life experiences up to that point had made him jaded to the ways of the world, but something told him that Em was sincere, and she would keep her promise.

Mike and Em continued their walk home, and as the night grew longer, it also grew colder. Mike could see that Em was cold, but was trying to play it off. He took off his hoodie and gave it to Em to wear.

Em smelled Mike's cologne on the hoodie and was struck by it. She knew she'd found a new scent that would forever be tied to a memory.

Em and Mike could feel the tension of a budding romance between them, but neither one of them dared to take the first step.

Mike thought, *I wish I could kiss her. She is magnificent in every way possible. She is cold; maybe if I bring her close, I can steal a kiss on the cheek. That's not too forward, and maybe it would set me up for something more.*

Em could see that Mike was anxious. She could read it in his face that he wanted a kiss as much as she did. Only, she hid it better because she was not stoned. She smiled a soft smile at Mike and inched her way closer to him until she was nestled comfortably inside his arms. She thought, *Wow, he wears such baggy clothes; I never realized how muscular he is. But, then again, that makes sense, given the sports he plays.*

As they continued on and approached Em's house, she asked, "Mike...?"

"Yes, Em?"

"What would you do if I asked you to kiss me?"

Mike's heart began to race. "U-Um...we-well..." Mike stuttered.

Em rushed in quickly and kissed Mike before he could say anything else. Mike grabbed Em close around her waist and lifted her ever so slightly. They stood there, lost in each other's arms, for what seemed like a lifetime.

Mike finally pulled away as he felt his watch buzzing. He checked the time, although he knew it was midnight since his watch was set to vibrate then.

Em stated, "Do you have to go? My parents aren't home. They went away for the weekend."

Mike instantly felt a wave of disappointment come over him. This was something he'd wanted since he met Em. And now, the opportunity had presented itself, but he had to decline. "Em, I would love nothing more than to come in, but, one, you have a boyfriend. And I don't want or need to start drama here. I can't express how much I want to come in and take you up on that offer, but I can't."

"Well, what's two?" Em asked.

"What's two, what?"

"Usually, when someone says 'one,' there is always a two," Em answered.

"I just started seeing someone from Ryder. We met a few weeks ago, and I really like her. I don't want to bring that drama into your life."

Em's face shifted from serenity to ambivalence as she pulled away quickly. "I didn't know you were dating someone."

"Yeah. Well, it's only been a week. But I really like her."

Mike knew he should stay with Em. He knew that the decision he was making right then would forever change his life. He prayed that he was making the right one by walking away, but deep down he knew that he was not.

"Em, the kiss we shared is forever imprinted on my mind and soul. I will never forget it as long as I live. But I do need to go. If the stars align, we will be together, but until then, this kiss is all we can share."

"Mike, I understand. I wish you the best of luck with who you are dating. Hopefully, the moon and stars will align, and we can see where we end up. Good night, Mike."

"Good night, Em, sweet dreams." Mike turned around to walk home.

Em watched him as he walked away. She called out, "Mike"—he turned around—"where are you going?"

"I passed the turn to my house two streets ago, but kept walking because I didn't want my time with you to end."

Em shook her head and said, "The moon and stars— remember that."

Bewildered, Mike repeated, "Moon and stars?"

Em clarified, "We will be together when the moon and stars align."

Mike nodded his head and replied, "Okay. Until the moon and stars align." He put his headphones back on, turned back around, and walked home.

Off in the alleyway, with the car's lights turned off and its motor running, shadowy figures rustled about inside a vehicle.

"Quiet down, dipshits," a voice states.

"'Ey, brother, isn't that the new kid leaving your girl's house?" asked another person inside the car.

Ronnie appeared from the shadows, his face illuminated by the streetlamp overhead. "You're fucking right, Tommy. I guess I'mma have to show that beaner a lesson," Ronnie stated. He grabbed the joint being passed around in the car, took a long hit, and stared as Mike turned the corner and disappeared into the night.

Chapter 6

As the school year progressed, Mike and Em passed each other in the halls and exchanged flirtatious pleasantries. Which led to playful brushing of each other's hair. Which then led to light touching of the hands. But nothing that would cross the line and give Ronnie a cause to feel challenged.

On the last day of their junior year, the school was buzzing with excitement about the completion of the school year and plans for the summer. Mike made his way to his locker, where he found Em waiting for him. He smiled and stated, "I see you are cutting class now."

Em giggled and responded, "Wwwweeeelll, there is only one person I would cut class to see."

Mike flashed his crooked, mischievous grin and said, "Oh, you went to see Ronnie? How is he? I bet his summer is gonna be chock-full of slapping his buddies' butts and then jumping on their balls?"

Em scoffs, giving Mike a stern look, and replies, "No! Wow, you're such an ass."

Mike's grin widens as he retorts, "I know. It's part of my charm."

Em rolls her eyes and says, "No, silly. I'd cut class for you. There's a lot of things I would do for you, but nobody else. But the reason I'm here waiting on you is cuz I know that after school you take off, and I wanted to catch you to see if maybe you wanted to sign my year-book. And maybe you'd want me to sign yours."

"Em, you know I don't like adhering to social con-formities. You've known me this whole year, and you haven't figured out that I'm anti-norm? I don't believe in the status quo. I live the motto of 'Rage against the machine.' What makes you think that I would buy a yearbook?"

Em looked down in humility and said, "I know. I just thought that maybe you would for me. I did ask you to get one when they were being sold."

"Well, your faith in me might have been misplaced." Mike opened his locker and continued, "But you can write all your feelings and thoughts about it in my yearbook."

Em's face lights up, and she jumps up and hugs Mike.

He instinctively grabs her and leans forward, pinning their embraced bodies against the lockers and preventing them from falling to the ground.

"Ggrrrr! Dammit, Mike, you are such an asshole," Em stated jokingly.

"Well, never mind. I'll put this back and see if I can get my money back. After all, it doesn't have any writing in it," Mike answered as he began to put the yearbook away.

Em's face was glowing with excitement at knowing that Mike bought the yearbook for her and only her. She quickly replied, "No, no, no. Give it to me." She snatched the yearbook from Mike and began feverishly writing.

After a few minutes, Em handed Mike back his yearbook and said, "Don't read it until tomorrow. Promise."

Mike reluctantly answered, "I promise."

Ronnie enters the hallway and witnesses Mike and Em hugging as they said their goodbyes. He rushes over and blindsides Mike, pushing him into the lockers.

Mike recovers from the shove and lowers his center of gravity, preparing to gut punch Ronnie with all his might. Mike stops at the last second as Em places herself between Ronnie and him.

Em cries out, "Ronnie, fucking stop it. Leave him alone."

Ronnie's left arm makes a large, swooping circle, over and around Em. He pushes her to the floor as he charges at Mike with perfect tackling form.

Mike steps aside and backs away. "Dude, chill the fuck out! Do you really want to spend your last day at school in the fucking hospital? I'll fuck you up," Mike yells.

The crowd in the hallway begin to chant, "Fight! Fight. Fight!"

As they form a huge circle around Mike and Ronnie, Mike dodges the few punches Ronnie throws. Judging from his fighting stance and the way he throws his punches, Mike knows that Ronnie does not have any real fighting experience.

"Look, dude. I don't know what you think you saw or what you think is going on, but Em and I are just friends. That's it," Mike declared.

"Fuck that shit, bitch. I saw you two the night of Homecoming. I know something is going on. I know you're fucking her. Leave her alone, you fucking spic motherfucker. Go back to Mexico, you fucking wetback."

Mike started laughing, infuriating Ronnie further, and stated, "You's a dumb motherfucker. No wonder you repeated a grade twice." Mike stretches out his arms, spins around, and proclaims, "All this land used to be Mexico, and before that, the Natives', you ignorant hillbilly. This *is* my land. This *is* my people's land. You go back to where you came from, you pussy motherfucker."

An enraged Ronnie charged at Mike with his full force.

Mike managed to escape Ronnie's lunge as Mr. Russ, the football coach, broke through the human ring and grabbed Ronnie, pinning him to the wall.

"Ronnie, stop that shit right now. You go after him again, you're off the team next year!" Mr. Russ yelled.

Ronnie stops glaring at Mike and focuses on Mr. Russ. He pulls away from the coach and says, "Fine. I'm going." He turns to Mike and says, "But this ain't over, bitch."

Mike turns around, throws his arms out, and replies, "Anytime you want to fuck with death, I'm right here. Bring it, motherfucker."

"C'mon, Milly. Let's go," Ronnie ordered.

Em sheepishly leaves with Ronnie. She turns around briefly to look at Mike and whispers, "I'm sorry."

Mike shakes his head and mouths, *"Me too."* Then he makes his way out of the school and heads home.

Chapter 7

Mike opens the yearbook and rereads the note Em inscribed in it.

To: Mike

This year was the best year of my life. Even though we didn't have classes together or get to spend much time with one another, the walks home we shared and the little notes meant the world to me. I hope next year I get to spend more time with you and see our friendship bloom. Stay cool. Stay the same.

Love,

Em

It's that last part that toyed with Mike's mind. *Love. What did she mean by that? A platonic love like the one you have for a sister? Or a deeper love? Like, you know, love, love?* This question plagued Mike all summer. Mike tried calling Em to ask her, but she kept avoiding his calls. Not knowing the answer led eventually to his breaking up with Sara, the girl he'd dated during his junior year.

One summer's day, Mike saw Em walk in to Braum's Burger Joint, where he worked for the summer. He spotted her first, and his heart skipped a beat even though Ronnie walked in right behind her. The feeling of excitement was short-lived, however. It was replaced by visceral rage when he spotted the black eye Em tried to cover up with makeup and the way she wore her hair.

Mike thought, *This motherfucker is gonna die. He is too scared to fight a real man and takes his anger out on those smaller than him. Oh hell no. He's gonna die today.*

Mike heard Ronnie shout, "Hey, babe. I'm gonna go piss. Order me a number seven with no onions."

Em makes her way to the counter and sees Mike standing there. She gasps and asks, "Mike, what are you doing here?"

"I work here. The real question is what happened to your eye? Did he give that to you?"

Em looks down at the counter, ashamed that Mike is seeing her like this.

"Is this the reason you haven't been answering my calls? And why you've been avoiding me?"

Em replies, "Mike, leave it alone. Don't say anything. I can handle it."

Mike is torn with emotions. He wants to end Ronnie, and he is mad at Em for not telling him this was going on.

"Mike! Promise me you won't say anything. Promise me," Em pleaded.

Mike nodded hesitantly and rang up her order.

As Em was paying, Ronnie appeared and stated, "Well…well…well…look what we have here. Is this why you wanted to come here, you fucking slut? You knew he was working here, and you wanted to see your fuck buddy?"

Mike clenched his fists and felt his ears turn bright red.

"Oh look, the beaner is now a red man. What you gonna do, red bean?"

Mike took a deep breath and said, "The total is twenty-three dollars and fifty-six cents."

Ronnie answers, "Well, pay your fuck buddy, girl."

Em looks down at the counter. Refusing to make eye contact with Mike, she gives him her debit card and then walks away with Ronnie.

Chapter 8

Mike's senior year seemed to be off to a good start. Mike was able to earn enough money to buy his first car. His relationship with Sara was rekindled, and things seemed to be going his way. Even though things were going well for Mike, he could not shake the feeling that this year would be unforgettable.

Mike walked into his first class, and there, sitting in the room, was Em. Mike looked at her and then took a seat at the back of the class, far away from Em.

Em paused for a moment, then grabbed her belongings, walked over, and sat next to Mike. "Excuse me, but can I sit here?" she asked.

Mike, staring straight ahead, replied, "It's a free country. As long as Ronnie approves, I guess you can sit there."

Em snapped back, "He has nothing to do with this. And I knew you were an asshole, but I didn't think you would be one to me."

Mike realized that he really was being an asshole to Em. He didn't mean to be, but he was confused and upset about their encounter over the summer. And he was still wondering about her inscription in his yearbook.

"Em, I'm sorry. It's just that you seriously fucked with my head. You wrote me that note in my yearbook, then dodged my calls, and later showed up at my job with a black eye. And now you act as if nothing happened. C'mon, Em, like, what the fuck?"

Em shyly looks down and answers, "About that, Mike...a lot of things happened over the summer. I just want to forget about it. As for Ronnie, well...uh...we broke up. He changed."

Mike's ears perk up at hearing that Em and Ronnie are no longer a couple. But the feeling quickly passes when he remembers that Sara and he are dating.

"So...I was wondering if, you know, maybe we could see what happens between us?" asked Em.

Mike rubbed the back of his head and said, "The moon and stars haven't aligned yet."

"What?"

"About a week ago, Sara and I got back together. She realized that the football player she liked was only using her to get to one of her friends."

Em looks at Mike in disgust, shaking her head, and says, "Are you stupid or something? She got back with you because the guy she liked didn't like her back. Do you really want to be with someone that will not make you a priority in their life—"

Interrupting, Mike says, "Like Ronnie did you?"

After Em gives Mike a look of shock and hurt, she answers, "Damn, Mike, just when I thought you couldn't get any lower—"

The teacher walks into the classroom and shouts, "Okay, students, take your seats."

Em leaves the desk next to Mike and sits in the front of the class.

Mike sits in the back of the class, sulking and replaying the conversation he and Em just had. His stomach turns, and he feels his ears turn red as he thinks about how he acted.

The rest of the day was a blur. In fact, the rest of the school year was torture for Mike. Em was in four of his seven classes, and in each class, they avoided each other. But each passed hopeful glances when the other was not looking. Mike often thought to himself that this is what Tantalus must have felt when he was cast out of the heavens.

Over the course of the school year, Mike heard that Em and Ronnie had started dating again. The news crushed Mike, and he started acting out in school and in his homelife. This cycle continued until prom.

Chapter 9

The evening of prom came. In the center of their living room, Maria and Tomas surround Mike and Sara. Mike is dressed in a midnight-blue, pin-striped zoot suit; Sara, in a red sequin dress.

Tomas says, "Look at you two. Such an amazing couple."

Mike responds, "Dad, stop it; you're embarrassing me."

Sara says sweetly, "Aw, thank you, Mr. P., I think we make a cute couple too."

Maria adds, "*Mira los dos, tan chulo*. You behave, okay? And be safe. I will light a candle for you two."

Jose enters the room and says, "Damn, Mike. I didn't know shit could look this good."

Tomas and Maria both yell, "Jose! That wasn't nice. Go to your room."

Sara comes to Mike's defense and says, "I think he looks *muy guapo*," and acts as if she were going to bite Mike.

Mike responds to Jose's comment with, "You wish you could look an eighth of how good I look."

Jose counters with, "Whatever. We all know I got the looks, and you got the ugly."

Mike shoots Jose a piercing look, one that Jose knows all too well.

"And with that, Ladies and Gentlemen, I'm gonna go to my room," Jose calls out as he makes his exit.

Mike and Sara take their pictures with Mike's parents and leave to make their way to the prom.

Miles pass before Sara says to Mike, "You could at least act like you are excited."

Mike stops staring at the road ahead and looks at Sara. "Huh?"

"Are you even excited to be going to the prom with me?"

"Where the fuck is this coming from? You wanted to go to prom. We are going. You wanted to have an after-party; we are going to an after-party. What more do you want from me?"

Sara huffed and said, "You haven't complimented me on how good I look or said anything about my hair—nothing."

Mike was flabbergasted, but she was right. Mike's mind was not on prom or Sara, or the after-party. He was thinking about seeing Em with Ronnie at prom. Mike was unsure of how he would act if he ran into them, especially after seeing what Ronnie did to Em over the summer.

"Mike, where are you?"

Mike shook his head, looked at Sara, and said, "I'm here with you, babe. And you're right. I haven't complimented you on how amazing you look. I just have a lot on my mind with finals and waiting on admission letters. I'm just stressin', and I don't really know how to handle it."

Sara slid over and said, "Well, baby, if you are stressin' so much, tell me. I know how to help you not stress so bad."

Sara begins to unzip Mike's pants and pull out his member. She grabs it and begins stroking it until he is close to release. She feels him getting firmer and engorged; then she wraps her lips around his member and swallows every drop as he releases.

Mike and Sara arrived at the Shriners' hall where prom was being held, and they were met by a few of the people Mike hung out with. They said their pleasantries and entered the room where the dance was being held. Over the next hour or so, Mike and Sara talked with people they knew and danced to a few songs.

Later, a voice rang out over the loudspeakers, "Attention, please. Attention, please. Good evening, Class of 2002. It is finally that time you have all been waiting for. It is time to announce this year's king and queen."

Mike's heart dropped. Deep down, he knew what the results would be.

"DJ, drumroll, please," the announcer called. This was followed by an automated drumroll. "This year's king and queen are...Ronnie Bagsby and Emily Sanchez. Will the king and queen please make their way to the stage to receive their crowns?"

The dance hall lit up with cheers from everyone—everyone except Mike—as Ronnie and Em made their way to the stage. Sara looked at Mike and saw the look of disgust on his face.

The announcer presented Ronnie and Em their crowns and then said, "Will the king and queen please make their way to the center of the dance floor for their dance?"

Em and Ronnie took each other's hands as they made their way to the dance floor. They embraced each other and began to slow dance to the music playing over the speakers.

As the song played on, more and more couples took to the dance floor. Eventually, Mike and Sara, also, made their way there. As they slow danced in a small circle, Mike's gaze was fixated on Ronnie and Em.

Sara followed Mike's stare and asked, "So that's her?"

Mike replied, "What? What are you talking about?"

"When we first got together, I always felt like there was someone else. Like you were with me, but deep down you wanted to be with someone else. And now I know who. Her…Emily."

Mike shook his head in disagreement and said, "Sara, you don't know what you are talking about. Em and I are just friends. You are the one I want to be with. I'm here with you, aren't I?"

Sara stares at Mike in disbelief and says, "I wish you would look at me the same way you look at her. You can't deny it, Mike. I see the way you look at her. It's obvious that you love her—"

Interrupting, Mike states, "Look, Sara, there is nothing there. Now, quit with your bullshit."

Sara's jaw drops in shock. "You know what, Mike? Fuck you! I don't need to be here with you. I have someone that wants to be with me for me. You're a piece of shit." She storms off the dance floor, leaving Mike alone.

Sara's actions catch the attention of Em.

Ronnie sees her looking in the direction of Sara and Mike and asks, "What the fuck you looking at?"

Taken aback by Ronnie's question, Em questions, "What are you talking about?"

Ronnie pulled Em closer and whispered, "You slut, you think you can play me? You think I'm fucking stupid? I know you are fucking him. I know it. You know it. The whole school knows it. You may think you're clever, but you're not. You make me look like an idiot."

Em's face went ghost white. She remembered what she'd endured over the summer.

The song ended, and Em left the dance floor to go to the bathroom to calm herself.

Mike saw Em make her exit, and he wanted to follow. He wanted to go to her side, profess his love, and tell her she didn't have to worry about Ronnie. But he did not. He decided that he would cause more problems for Em if Ronnie saw him do that.

The night ended, and even though Sara was gone, Mike decided he would go to the after-parties alone. He made his way to the DoubleTree Hotel, where one of them was occurring. Mike stayed for a few hours, but felt out of place, so he left and decided to head to the falls to clear his mind.

Chapter 10

Mike glances at his watch as he takes a big swig from his beer. The cool night air feels good on his face. While taking a big hit from his blunt, something catches his attention. Mike lies quietly and listens. The sound of soft crying piques his interest, so he gets up off the ground to investigate where it is coming from. As he gets closer to the source of the crying, he realizes that he recognizes the sound.

Mike peers through the bushes, and to his surprise, he sees Em sitting on the bench overlooking the falls.

"Em, are you okay?" Mike asked. He knew it was a dumb question because, if she were, she would not be crying alone at night.

Startled, Em quickly turned to look over her shoulder and asked, "Who's there?"

Mike came through the bushes and said, "Uh...um... Mike."

"Mike? What are you doing here?"

"I came here to clear my head and gather my thoughts. Sara left me at the prom, and I really didn't feel like partying. So I came here to be alone and smoke some weed. And think and be alone."

As Mike was coming around the bushes to sit next to Em, he saw her dress had been torn, and her makeup was smeared. He guessed that something had happened between Ronnie and her. He wanted to ask what happened, but knew better. He had seen enough to figure it out on his own.

"Mike...there are so many things I want to tell you. You don't know the hell I've been through. Ronnie—"

Mike stopped Em and said, "Em, it's obvious that something happened. I can see that you have gone through some things. I don't need to know, and you don't have to tell me if you don't want to. I just want you to know that you are safe now. I am here for you. I will always be here for you."

Em knew that Mike was sincere and that he would be there for her. She wanted to tell him how, over the summer, Ronnie mentally tortured her. How he forced her to have sex with him against her will. She wanted Mike to know that Ronnie got drunk regularly and, for no reason, hit her and told her she was a whore, a slut, and no one but he would want her.

But Em couldn't bring herself to tell Mike those things. She felt too ashamed and embarrassed. She thought that if she told him, he would think less of her.

Em tried to start again, "Mike—"

Again he interrupted and said, "Em, you don't have to say anything. We can just sit here and stare off into the distance."

Em broke down on Mike's shoulder, and Mike gently held her. They sat on the park bench overlooking the falls for hours, until Em started to yawn.

Mike suggested, "Em, it's getting late. Let's get out of here. I have a suite at the DoubleTree; you can sleep in the bed, and I'll take the couch."

Em nodded in agreement, and they left together.

* * *

In the hotel room, Mike let Em shower, clean herself up, and lent her his shirt to sleep in. He made his bed on the pullout couch and lit the logs in the fireplace. After that, Mike showered and lay down on the couch.

Em appeared in the doorway and said, "Mike…"

"Yeah?"

"Good night. And thank you for everything."

Mike smiled and responded, "Em, you don't need to thank me. And good night, my love."

Em's heart fluttered at hearing "my love." She turned and went to lie down on the queen-size bed in the other room.

Mike lay on the pullout couch and flipped through the TV channels for a bit before passing out. He awakened in the middle of the night as Em made her way onto the pullout couch.

"Em what are you doing?"

"I can't sleep. I felt so alone and scared in the other room. And I feel safe and comfortable in your arms. I just wanted to lay next to you."

"Okay." He scooted over on the pullout couch and made room for Em.

As they lie in each other's arms, Em whispers, "I love you, Mike."

Mike answers, "To the moon and stars," and kisses Em sweetly on her forehead. He pulls her in close and holds her tight as they both drift off to sleep.

Chapter 11

Mike wakes up and sees Em lying in his arms peacefully. The sunlight pokes through the hotel room's curtains at the correct angle, giving Em's perfect skin a soft glow. She gently repositions in bed. This shift allows Mike to slip out, leaving Em undisturbed. With his back to Em, he throws on his shirt, then turns and walks over to her, gently kisses her forehead, and lightly brushes her hair. Then he heads to the lobby.

Em was awakened as Mike got up and dressed. Watching Mike, Em realized that she had never seen him without his shirt. She gazed at his muscular body as the light shone in the room, emphasizing even the slightest definition of his physique. Em never knew that Mike had his entire back covered in tattoos.

Seeing that he was turning toward her, Em quickly closed her eyes. Her heart skipped a beat when she felt his soft, plump lips pressed upon her forehead. She felt a rush of emotions swell from deep within her. Em wanted to grab him, pull him into bed, and ravage him. Kiss every inch of his body, explore every twist and turn of it while he explored hers. She wanted to touch and tease him to the point that he would animalistically grab her and pleasure her until they both passed out from sheer passionate, physical exhaustion. However, she held back; she knew that the time was not right. She watched him exit the room and lay their waiting for him to return.

Mike returns to the room with two cups of coffee and sees the pullout sleeper empty, but hears movement in the other room.

Em calls out, "Mike is that you?"

"No, it's hotel security. We got complaints about a beautiful, dangerous woman staying in this room, capturing a man's heart, and holding it hostage."

Blushing, Em walks into the main room with a huge smile on her face. She floats to Mike, rests her hands on his chest, stands on her toes, and stretches up to Mike. She gets within an inch of his face, gazing deeply into his dark-brown eyes. Biting her lower lip, she whispers

"So, I have your heart, huh? Well, now that I am like a raccoon, I'm never gonna let it go. It's mine and will always be mine." Then she kisses Mike, taking his breath away.

Mike's whole body quivers so much he almost drops the coffee. Mike instinctively adjusts his body to keep from spilling the coffee; he then sets the cups down on the kitchenette's counter.

Em laughs at Mike's clumsiness as it was a side of him she'd never seen before. For as long as she had known Mike, he was always composed, calm, and sure of himself. Seeing this side of him deepened her affection for him.

"So...do all good-morning kisses do this to you, Mike?"

Mike smiles widely. Not his typical smart-ass grin, but a genuine smile that emphasized his dimples. Dimples Em had never noticed before; they caused her heart to flutter.

Mike answered while taking his right hand and rubbing the back of his head, "Um...uh, no. I...uh..."

Em quickly retorted, "I see. It's just me. It will always be me that can get you to be like this."

Mike broke his gaze and looked down at the floor, feeling unsure of himself. He rarely felt this way. Mike was unaccustomed to being insecure, and did not like it. But Em had a way of making him feel vulnerable and seen. In her presence, he felt both scared and safe, excited and frightful, but always at peace.

Peace was something that had evaded Mike for quite some time. Yet, being around Em, he had come to know the feeling of peace. There was just something about Em's aura that calmed him.

Mike glances at the clock and states, "Em, we need to get going. Checkout time is soon."

Em thought to herself that she didn't want this day to end. She just wanted to be safe in bed with Mike, wrapped in his arms, and feeling his body next to hers. She wanted this moment to last forever because, once they left, nothing would be promised.

Mike and Em checked out of the hotel and headed home. Mike walked to the passenger side of the car to open the door for Em.

"Oh, how chivalrous of you, but I am a modern woman. I can open my own door."

Mike quickly answered with his crooked grin, "I know, but the car door gets stuck, and Fiona doesn't like strange women riding in her; she throws temper tantrums."

Em laughs. "So your car's name is Fiona?"

Mike nodded his head as he opened the door, allowing Em to enter. "She is very protective of me," Mike said as he walked around to the other side and got in.

A few minutes into the drive, Em slides over on the bench seat and snuggles up next to Mike. She lays her head on his shoulder and takes his hand in hers. Em starts, "Mike, promise me that you will always be here for me."

Mike takes his eyes off the road and looks at Em. "Em, I will always be here for you. No matter what life throws at us, you can always count on me when you need anything."

Em smiles and kisses Mike on the cheek. They both sit in silence the rest of the drive home, snuggled up against one another.

Mike gets to Em's house and parks in the driveway. Em leans in for one more kiss from Mike. Mike holds Em, and, lightly touching her, they share a passionate kiss.

Em breaks away first, biting her lower lip and saying, "Call me later. Please?"

Mike answered, "I will."

Excitedly, Em exited the car and made her way to the house.

Mike watched Em walk to the top of the stairs.

She stopped, turned around, and ran back to steal another kiss. After that, she walked back to the door, turned one last time, and waved.

Mike smiled and waved back. Then drove off after she entered the house.

Chapter 12

As the school year came to a conclusion, Mike and Em's relationship grew. They were over the stars in love with each other. Although they never made their relationship official, everyone assumed they were together. Little did everyone know that they were just close friends. They would occasionally hold hands or share a kiss, but never let it cross into anything more.

As with any senior year, college applications had been sent earlier in the year, and now replies were starting to come in. Em was standing by Mike's locker after his last class. She lit up with excitement at the sight of Mike.

"Wow, you're happy to see me," Mike stated.

Em quickly pulled out a big envelope bearing the school crest of the University of Southern California. "Mike. Mike. Mike. It's big. It's big, Mike. You know what that means…right? Right?" Em squeaked.

Mike laughed at seeing the excitement in Em's face. She had been talking about going to USC since her junior year, and now it seemed as if it was becoming a reality.

"Did you open it?"

"No, silly. I was waiting for you. I wanted to share this moment with you."

"Well, what are you waiting for? Open it!" Mike said with excitement.

Em begins to read the letter loudly and confidently.

Dear Emily Sanchez,

We would like to thank you for your application to the University of Southern California. We have reviewed your application and…

Em's voice softened as her facial expression changed from excitement to disappointment. She kept reading, and her voice started to trail off.

Mike became concerned; he dreaded the thought that Em's dream had not come true. "Em," he started, "I'm sorry, love. I'm sorry that you didn't get in. You are better than that school."

Em looked up from the letter and said, "Well, you know what? It's not their loss 'cause I'm going to USC this fall!" Em screamed with joy.

Mike's crooked grin appeared again as he said, "Dammit, that was not funny. I was seriously sad and hurt for you!"

Em started laughing and replied, "It's cuz you love me," as she leaned in to give him a kiss. "Did you hear back from any of the schools you applied to?"

Mike replied nonchalantly, "I got accepted to the University of Miami, Duke, and the University of Texas. Not sure which one I'm going to. The way it looks right now, I'm gonna go to Miami since they are offering a full ride."

"Oh my God, Mike, that's great. Why are you not more excited?"

"Well, it's cuz…you know…I don't believe in social conformities."

Em rolled her eyes and said, "Oh, Mike, always the rebel."

* * *

School finally ended and summer took hold. Mike tried to spend as much time as possible with Em before she left on her family vacation. They saw each other at the pool and talked every day on the phone. The night before she left, Em insisted on seeing Mike face-to-face.

Mike and Em met at their spot in the park. Mike was early, so he laid out the blanket and waited for Em's arrival. Fifteen minutes past the agreed-upon meeting time of ten o'clock, Em finally showed up. Mike got up, excited he would get to see Em before she was gone for most of the summer.

"Em, did you have a hard time sneaking out?"

"No. Mike, this is going to be quick. I wanted to let you know that Ronnie's family is coming with us on vacation. And I wanted to tell you before you heard it from somewhere else."

Mike instantly was filled with rage at the thought that Ronnie would be that close to Em. Especially after all the traumatic things he did to her. "Em, you need to tell your parents how he treated you. You need to tell them the things he forced you to do. If they knew, they would not want you anywhere near that monster," Mike pleaded.

"Mike, I can handle it. And you know I can't tell my parents any of that. What would they think of me? How do you think that would go?"

"Em, they need to know," insisted Mike.

"Mike, leave it alone? Do you not trust me? Do you think I would let something happen? I love you. You are my world, my North Star, my guiding light. I would never put that at jeopardy. God, you are no better than Ronnie!" yelled Em.

Mike's face lit up with shock; his mouth dropped, and he gasped. "Don't you ever compare me to that mother-fucker. I have done my fair share of dirt, but I have never ever acted like that motherfucker. And, no, it's not that I don't trust you; I don't trust him. He has already beaten you, abused you, and treated you like you were trash… nothing…less than nothing. How dare you compare me to that prick," Mike proclaimed in anguish.

A moment of silence passed, and then Mike said, "Em, I am sorry." He reached over to hold her.

Em pulled away and said, "You know what, Mike… maybe it's good that we are going to schools at opposite ends of the country. Maybe we were just each other's Band-Aid."

Mike gets up and begins to walk away in silence. He takes a few slow steps, pauses, and feels the engage-ment ring he has in his pocket. The ring he worked so hard for the past year to save up for in order to propose to Em before they both went off to college.

He hoped she would call him back. He didn't want their relationship to end, especially not like this. But she never called him to come back, and he walked off a broken man. A shell of his former self. He knew that a part of him had died right then...and that he may never get it back.

Em stood there, watching Mike walk away. She tried to call him back, but the words would not come out. She wanted to run to Mike and hold him. She wanted to grab him and tell him, "Let's run away tonight and start a new life, just the two of us." But she couldn't. She was paralyzed with fear, but didn't know how to tell Mike that. She could not find the words to tell Mike that he was her everything and that, without him, she was nothing. She just stood there, watching the love of her life walk away. And she knew that she'd just lost Mike forever.

Chapter 13

There were three weeks left of the summer before Mike was set to leave for college. Two months had passed since he'd last spoken to Em, and his soul still ached from how things ended. Mike spent his summer in an endless loop of working, getting high, drinking, and fornicating with random women, attempting to fill the void left by Em, but nothing worked.

Mike often found himself alone and lost in his thoughts, replaying the way things ended. He thought about what he should have said. How he should have just swallowed his pride and professed his love to her.

One late-summer afternoon, Mike was working at Braum's when in walked Ronnie with a group of his friends. Mike's blood began to boil.

Ronnie sees Mike at the counter and shoots him a cocky smile as he walked up to the counter. "Well, look who it is. It's the fucking red bean," shouted Ronnie.

Mike stares Ronnie dead in the eyes with an expressionless face and says, "The fuck you want?"

Ronnie laughs, smiles, and says, "Whoa, whoa, bean. Is that how you're supposed to talk to the customers?"

Mike quickly shot back, "You're no customer. You're a piece-of-shit abuser of women and a rapist."

Ronnie's face turned beet red, and he started yelling, "What the fuck did you say to me? I don't know what that little bitch told you, but she wanted everything she got. She begged for it. Just like she did when we were on vacation. She couldn't get enough of my dick. Tell me, bean, did she tell you that we got back together? I bet she didn't. You lost, man. She is mine. Has been mine and will always be mine."

Mike's ears turned fiery red at hearing what Ronnie was saying. He responded, "Em is not something to possess, you misogynistic prick. She is a kind, loving soul that deserves way better than you. Let me find out that you hurt her, and I will end you. I will fucking end you!"

Letting out a bellowing laugh, Ronnie looks toward his friends and in a mocking tone says, "You hear that, guys. If anything ever happens to me, this red bean here will be the prime suspect. Wooooo, I'm so scared."

Mike regains his composure and says, "Listen, you guys need to buy something or leave."

Ronnie looks at Mike and then turns to his friends and says, "C'mon guys. I don't know about you, but I lost my appetite. Plus, judging by the people that work here, the food is probably all greasy." Ronnie and his group of friends head to the door to leave. As Ronnie exits the door, he turns around, gives Mike his two middle fingers, and mouths the words, *"Fuck you."*

Mike begins to spiral as he plays out different scenarios in his head. He knew better than to believe what Ronnie told him, but parts of him could not help but think it was true, especially after how things ended with Em. *Did she do it to get revenge on me? Was she just toying with me to use me as a play toy and discard me like a piece of trash? Mike thought to himself. No. No, it can't be. Em wouldn't do that. She is not that type of person.* Mike knew one thing. He had to see Em. He had to get answers.

Night fell, and Mike made his way over to Em's house. He climbed the side of the house Em's room was on and knocked on her window. Em, startled by the knock, came to the window and let Mike in.

As Em approached the window, Mike felt a visceral rage come over him. He saw that Em's face was black-and-blue and swollen. It was evident that she had been beaten.

"Mike, what are you doing here?" Em asked, surprised.

Mike calmly said, "I needed to see you. Did he do this to you?"

Em turned her head away in shame and embarrassment and nodded her head. She started sobbing and tried to explain, "One night, he was drunk and horny, and he came to my cabin. He started telling me he loved me and couldn't live without me. Then he started to kiss me. I pushed him off and told him he was drunk and needed to leave. I told him I didn't love him. I told him that I loved you, and only you, Mike. Then he slapped me, threw me on the bed, started to lift up my nightshirt and...and...and—"

Mike stopped her from continuing. "Sshhh. You don't have to tell me any more. I get it. What do you need from me? What did your parents say?"

"I tried to explain what happened and tell them what Ronnie did. But he explained it away. My parents are so blinded by his charm that they can't see the monster he is. To make matters worse, I'm pregnant with his child. Mike, I can't have his child. I can't have Ronnie tied to me for the rest of my life. Having his child would force me to give up all my dreams. I want children, but not like this. Not forced on me. All I want from you is to hold me. Stay with me and hold me."

Mike took Em into his arms and held her until she fell asleep. While waiting for Em to fall asleep, Mike reflected on all that she'd told him. He saw how distraught she was. How scared she was. Mike knew he had to do something. But what? What could he do? How could he help?

"Em? Em?" Mike whispered, seeing if she was asleep. Em repositioned slightly, giving Mike just enough room to get out of bed without waking her. He made his way to her dresser and scribbled a note to her on a piece of paper. Then he walked over to Em, kissed her softly and sweetly on her forehead, and whispered, "I love you, Em. Don't worry. Things will be all right."

Em awoke when Mike got out of bed. She saw him standing at her desk, writing something down. When she saw him turning to come toward her, she closed her eyes, pretending to be asleep. She was scared, but knew that Mike would make everything all right. Em lay awake the rest of the night, wondering what Mike was going to do.

Mike left Em's house and made his way to the old grain silo, assuming Ronnie would be there, doing the same things he usually did with his friends there. Mike hid in the shadows off in the distance. From his vantage point, he could only see Ronnie. Judging by his movements,

Mike knew Ronnie was in a pretty intoxicated state. Mike waited a few minutes, ensuring that Ronnie was alone.

"Ronnie!" Mike called out.

Ronnie turned around to look at Mike and was met with a barrage of fists. Mike hit Ronnie square in the nose, causing his eyes to tear up. That was followed by a quick uppercut to the gut, knocking the wind out of Ronnie. Mike continued his attack with hits to the temple, then groin, then ribs and knees. Mike's whole goal was to inflict as much pain as he could without actually killing Ronnie.

"Yeah, not so tough now, are you, fucker? You can't handle someone your own size. You like picking on helpless women."

Ronnie's body fell to the ground, landing on his back. Mike knelt over him, grabbed him by the collar, and repeatedly punched Ronnie in the face. Blood poured out of Ronnie's mouth as he gasped for air.

Mike finally came to a stop as Ronnie started slipping in and out of consciousness. Mike stood up and said, "This is your one and only warning. If you ever hurt Em again…if I hear you mention her name…I will kill you. Do you understand me? I will fucking kill you!"

Ronnie managed to nod.

Mike threw one last punch to Ronnie's face to emphasize his sincerity. He started to walk away and leave Ronnie a bloody mess on the ground.

Ronnie coughs a few times and manages to say, "You know…when…I had…that little bitch…bent over the bed…she was crying…and calling out for you. She said, 'No, please don't. Mike, help me. Mike, save me.' And I told her that you wouldn't do shit. That you were a little wetback that would fail her and didn't want her. That you would never come for her. She was mine to do anything I wanted to with."

Mike stopped in his tracks and clenched his fists. His whole body was shaking in reaction to what Ronnie had just said. Mike let out a primal scream and heard a loud ringing in his ears.

Instantly, Mike's vision went black. He heard nothing…felt nothing…saw nothing.

* * *

Two weeks later…

A woman notices a pack of coyotes hanging around her old barn. A loud shotgun round echoes, scaring the coyotes off. The woman enters the barn and lets out a horrified scream. Hanging from the center of the barn is the lifeless body of a man. The woman hurries out of the barn and calls the police.

The local police come and secure the crime scene. They tape off the barn, and the crime-scene investigators cut down the body. A police officer named Hector Gomez takes the statement from the woman.

The woman asked, "What do you think happened?"

Officer Gomez answered, "My initial impression is that the man committed suicide. But we will know more about what happened once forensics does their job and after we find out who the person is."

Back at the police station, Officer Gomez is sitting at his desk, looking over the little evidence he has on his new case. Lost in thought, Officer Gomez keeps muttering to himself, "Who are you? Who are you?"

The computer on his desk starts beeping; it snaps Officer Gomez back to the present. A picture of Ronnie is front and center on his computer monitor.

"Huh. Well, now we know who you are. We just need to find out what happened to you, Mr. Ronnie Bagsby," said Officer Gomez.

* * *

Meanwhile in Oklahoma City...

A man in a uniform is standing in the front of a poorly lit room.

Mike thinks to himself, *I can't believe I am here. I said I would never be here. And fucking here I am,* as he is led to the center of the room and asked to stand under a spotlight.

The man says, "Raise your right hand, and repeat after me."

Mike raises his right hand and repeats, "I, Michael Perez, do solemnly swear that I will support and defend the Constitution of the United States against all enemies, foreign and domestic; that I will bear true faith and allegiance to the same; and that I will obey the orders of the President of the United States and the orders of the officers appointed over me, according to regulations of the Uniform Code of Military Justice, so help me God."

The man looks at Mike, extends his right hand, and says, "Well, son. Welcome to the Army. Grab your bags and get on the bus. Your next stop is Fort Benning, Georgia, home of the infantry."

Mike grabs his bags and heads to the bus; he stops at the first step and looks over at his bruised hand, which is gripping the railing. Mike's thoughts drift to Em, and he mutters to himself, "I kept my promise."

Then Mike gets on the bus, takes his seat, puts on his headphones, hits Play, and chuckles slightly. *Well, this is a fitting song.* He closes his eyes and falls asleep.

Chapter 14

Vanessa sits at Mike's bedside, replaying the last words she spoke to him before his injury. *"I'm not sure how much longer I can do this. I'm tired of being alone. I'm tired of you being gone. You are not the same person you were when we met. When you get back, we can give it one more try. But if things don't change, then I am done."*

She now wonders if their last conversation was the reason he ended up here. Did their fight distract him, make him lose focus, and lead to his injury? When she got the call from Chris, letting her know Mike was injured, she'd thought he was joking. She didn't believe him and told him to stop playing. Then, listening to the trembling in his voice and how he was choking down his tears, she knew it was real.

Since this was Vanessa's second deployment with Mike, she knew that whenever a serious injury occurred, they shut down all communication back to the United States until notification could be made to the family members. So if Chris was calling to tell her, then it meant that it must have happened recently and that he was breaking protocol by calling and telling her.

Vanessa remembered that she was only able to ask, *"Is he...?"*

Chris had responded, trying to swallow his emotions, *"I...don't...know. I...did...my...best...Vanessa. I tried...my... best."* Vanessa could hear Chris breaking down and start crying on the other end of the phone. She feared the worst.

Vanessa knew that Chris and Mike had deployed once before when they'd taken heavy casualties. Hearing Chris this shaken up only heightened her fears. Before either one could get another word out, the phone line had gone dead.

"Excuse me, Mrs. Perez," a nurse said, interrupting Vanessa's mental spiral. "Um, it's shift change, and I will be leaving soon. This is Susan; she will be taking care of Mike today."

Vanessa looked up at the day nurse and said, "Good morning. I don't need anything. I will do my best to stay out of the way."

"Okay, ma'am. Well, if you need anything, let me know," Nurse Susan said.

Vanessa spent most of her days at Mike's bedside. As far as she knew, Em had never come back to see Mike after their last interaction. Vanessa wanted to know if that was true, but she did not ask the medical staff because, deep down, she did not really want to know the answer. Knowing would make it real...and would reopen a wound that was still very fresh.

* * *

Days merged into weeks, and weeks turned into months. Mike's condition remained unchanged, as did Vanessa's routine. Each morning, she woke up and checked on Logan, Jami, and Lexi to make sure they were doing okay and behaving for Mike's parents. Then she did a light workout, grabbed breakfast and coffee, got dressed, checked in with her job, and made her way to the hospital. At the hospital, Vanessa met with the team of nurses and doctors who watched over Mike; then she sat back, settling into her watch-and-wait routine—watching over and waiting for the love of her life to regain consciousness.

Despite what he had done, she loved him. His betrayal still weighed heavily on her mind. *How long has this been going on? How does Em know my name? Why did Mike do this?* A whirlwind of whys and hows constantly flooded Vanessa's mind.

While staring off into space and trying to navigate the questions on which she was ruminating, a toy plane on Mike's bedside table catches Vanessa's eye, and she begins to examine it. The plane looks out of place. She gets up, makes her way over to the toy, picks up the plane, and studies it for a moment. It reminds her of a toy with which her son used to play. A toy that Mike gave Logan on his second birthday.

The pit of Vanessa's stomach turns and wrenches. Her face flushes, and her knees get weak. Deep down, she knows that the owner of that toy has to be related to Mike. It cannot be a coincidence; there are thousands of toys, but to have that plane be so similar to the one Mike gave Logan... The circumstances had to be the same.

Right then and there, Vanessa decided that she must get the answers to the questions she had been avoiding. She must know the extent of Em and Mike's relationship.

Vanessa waited until the end of normal visiting hours; then she went downstairs to the cafeteria and drank some coffee, waiting to see if Em would show up to see Mike. She waited until midnight before making her way back to Mike's room. As she approached the nurses' station, she saw the look of surprise on the staff's faces; she knew Em was there.

Vanessa waved pleasantly and said, "I'm just gonna pop in and see my husband. I'll be in and out quickly."

A nursing-staff member managed to say, "Okay."

As Vanessa approaches the room, she can see a shadowy figure illuminated by the hospital monitors. Vanessa opens the door...

Em gasps and looks directly into Vanessa's eyes. An uneasy silence fills the room, and time slows. It felt as if an eternity had passed between those seconds.

Vanessa feels her face and ears flush. Her heart beats faster; her fists clench. The sight of Em still enrages Vanessa, but she takes a few calming breaths, closes her eyes, and tries to clear her mind. She opens her eyes, reaches into her purse, pulls out the toy airplane, and finally speaks. "Is the owner of this toy his child?" Vanessa asks as she points to Mike.

Em hesitates for a second before nodding. "But I want to explain—"

"No, I don't want to hear it," Vanessa says, stopping Em in midsentence. She then unloads a barrage of questions. "Who are you? How did you even meet my husband? Did you know that he had a wife and kids? If you did, why did you fuck my husband? What promise are you keeping?"

Em silently waits, allowing Vanessa to finish. Then she takes a deep breath and answers, "My name is Emily. I have known Mike for the better part of ten years. We went to school together, and he was my best friend—"

Vanessa interrupted again, "Just friends?"

"Yes, just friends. Although I would be lying to you if I said I didn't want it to be something more. But...that never happened."

Em paused for a moment and then continued, "I didn't know he had a family." Em felt her face flush with shame. "I didn't know. But I assumed he did. Mike is the type of guy that can make anyone fall head over heels for him. He has a way of making you feel seen and heard. When I was going through a dark time in my life, he was there to make me feel safe. He made me feel like I was the only person in the world. When no one would listen to me, and I was on the verge of ending my own life, he pulled me back from the edge."

Vanessa could feel the hatred inside begin to subside. She wanted to hate Em for what she did, but she could not help but relate to her. Mike did have a way of making a person feel seen. Vanessa thought about how Mike and her met, and how, when she looked into his eyes, she felt vulnerable, but yet, at the same time, safe.

Vanessa had heard what Em said so far, but Em's words had not fully calmed Vanessa's emotions. In her mind, Vanessa tried to vilify Em, but could not because she saw a part of herself in Em. Plus, she now had to consider an innocent child.

Em continued, "I want you to know that I don't want anything from Mike or you. I don't want to take Mike from you. I make plenty of money, so I don't need child support. I just want Mike to have the opportunity to know his son, and our son to know his father."

Hearing Em say "our son" made Vanessa's blood boil. The thought of Mike having a child with another woman enraged her. Vanessa could not fathom her husband fathering another child.

Vanessa closed her eyes and tried to center herself. After a few seconds, she opened her eyes and began to speak. "I am filled with so much emotion, and I have even more questions. I am so mad I don't even know where to begin. For now, I will let you see Mike so that your son can see his father. I am not a monster who punishes an innocent child for the mistakes of his parents. But as for me and you…we should still stay away from each other."

Em nods her head in agreement.

Vanessa and Em come to an uneasy agreement about visiting Mike. Vanessa grabs her things, looks back at Em, who is sitting at Mike's bedside, and leaves the hospital room.

Chapter 15

Em sits quietly at Mike's bedside, holding his hand and resting her head on Mike's arm, looking up at him. Lost in her own thoughts, Em mumbles to herself, "God, I hope you are okay. Please come back to me." Em grasps Mike's hand tighter as tears begin to flow silently from her eyes.

Em looks up at the clock and starts to gather her things; it was almost 0600 and she knew that Vanessa would be coming by soon to be with Mike. She didn't want to leave, but knew that she must. The uneasy alliance they had forged was a spark away from burning them all to the ground if Em crossed Vanessa.

She also knew she needed to get home because *he* would be waiting for her. At only eighteen months old, Miguel was the spitting image of Mike. Seeing Miguel every day was torture for Em; he was a constant reminder of the man she could never have.

Em makes her way to the elevator, lost in thought about all the things she needs to accomplish that day. The elevator doors open, and standing there is Vanessa. Vanessa's smiling face quickly turns to a mean scowl as Em looks away and clenches her belongings.

Vanessa makes her way out of the elevator and purposely bumps into Em. "Watch where you're walking," Vanessa says forcefully.

The bump caused Em to drop her belongings. She scurries to pick up her belongings from the hospital floor. As she bends down, Em drops to her knees and begins sobbing uncontrollably, burying her face in her hands.

Vanessa witnesses Em's horrible breakdown. The scene causes Vanessa to stop and reconnect with her humanity. She walks back to Em and begins to help her pick up her stuff.

"Hey, look...I'm sorry I was a bitch just now. I didn't mean for you to drop your stuff," Vanessa said. "I didn't know my actions would have this kind of effect on you. What's really bothering you?"

Em looks at Vanessa with tear-soaked eyes and answers, "Why do you care? Why does it even matter? To you, I'm just the other woman. The one that fucked your husband and is trying to ruin your life. Why should how I feel or what I'm going through matter to you?"

Vanessa pauses for a moment, reflecting on what Em just said. *Why do I care about how the woman that slept with my husband feels? Why should I care about what she is going through?*

Vanessa begins, "To be honest, I don't care. It really doesn't matter to me what is going on with you or your life. If I had it my way, you wouldn't be allowed to see Mike."

Em begins crying violently after hearing Vanessa berate her. *She is right; Vanessa has the moral high ground here, after all. Mike's and my indiscretions have emotionally devastated Vanessa. If only I could talk to her. If only Vanessa knew the truth about Mike and his feelings toward her.*

"Vanessa, look, I get it. You hate me," Em manages to say between tears. "In your eyes, I am the one that ruined your marriage. I am the one that stole your man from you. But if you only knew the truth. Mike knew more about you than you think. Mike knew what you were hiding. I feel like shit. I feel worse than that. I am the one that loves a man that I can never really have. I love a man that cares about people so deeply that he would give his life for them."

Em could see the look of superiority on Vanessa's face fade to one of shock and fear.

"What do you mean, Mike knew more than I thought? You don't know what you are talking about. You are just trying to deflect your guilt to me. I did not do anything."

Vanessa's gut churned; there was some truth to what Em was saying. *Does Mike really know about Robert and me? It was a brief fling, and it didn't mean anything. Not like him and Em. Mike and I were on a break. We didn't know if we were going to be together anymore.* Vanessa shakes off thoughts of the past.

Em caught the flash of fear in Vanessa's eyes. She knew that there was truth to what she was saying. "So it *is* true," Em states.

Vanessa gasps and shakes her head. "No. You don't know what you are talking about."

Em continued, "Mike knew. So don't stand there on your moral high ground. You did what you did. And now you stand there, casting judgment on me and Mike. Go fuck yourself. I don't need your shit right now."

Em snatched her belongings from Vanessa's hands and made her way to the stairs. Em was not about to suffer the indignity of Vanessa's condescending words. She knew that, despite Mike's knowing about Vanessa's torrid affair, he still loved her and wanted to make things work.

She wished that he felt that way about her. She hoped that one day she could have Mike to the same degree that Vanessa captivated him.

She closes her eyes tightly and tears quietly fall. Her mind drifts back to a few months prior to the last conversation she had with Mike. Back to when she told him she was pregnant…and the lie she told Mike after that.

Chapter 16

Fifteen months earlier…

Em looks over the email one last time before she hits Send.

I should wait until he gets back. He doesn't need this drama in his life. Not now. Mike just needs to focus on what he has to do to get back home.

Em tries to recall or delete the message, but she is unsuccessful.

* * *

In a distant but familiar land, Mike is just getting back from a three-day mission as the HMMWVs pull into the motor pool. Sergeant First Class Miller shouts, "'Ey, Doc, what ya gonna do now that we made it back?"

Mike responded, "Same thing I always do when I get back. I'm gonna check with Lucas at the aid station to make sure none of the other medics got hit. Then a nice warm shower, shitty DFAC food, and a good night's sleep after rubbing one out to the old lady."

Sergeant Miller smiled and said, "Damn, Doc, didn't need to know all that. I was just wondering if you wanted to jam on some Guitar Hero."

Mike laughed and answered, "Maybe after my rub-and-tug and a nap."

"So, like, in thirty-three minutes?"

Mike gave Miller a confused look and said, "Thirty-three minutes?"

"Yeah, it will take you about five minutes to check in at the aid station. Another ten to shower and change. Two minutes to beat off, one minute to fall asleep. That leaves you with enough time for a fifteen-minute nap before I spank that ass in Guitar Hero."

Mike smiled and answered, "Damn, Big Sarge, you give me too much credit. Two minutes is my best showing. Right now, I'd be lucky if I lasted fifteen seconds. But, yeah, give me about thirty-five minutes, and I'll be ready for some Guitar Hero."

Sergeant Miller smiles, nods his head, and says, "Bet."

Mike grabs his weapon, backpack, and head covering, and makes his way to the aid station to check in with Lucas. Mike knocks on the faded white doors and shouts, "'Ey, douche, you in here?" Mike opens the door slowly and makes his way in, shouting again, "Lucas? You in here?"

The aid station is eerily quiet for noon. Mike grabs the pistol that is holstered at the side of his right hip and shouts one last time, "Lucas, you here, bud?"

As Mike makes his way to the back supply area, he hears muffled moans and a familiar, thick Puerto Rican accent say, "Oooh, yeah, Mami, *dámelo así.*"

Mike made his way to the door to the room from which the sounds were coming. Leaning his head softly against the door, he could hear the sounds of sex emanating more clearly. He smiles and tries to guess which desert queen was in there with Lucas.

Mike quickly looked for the Super Soaker that was kept in the aid station. He filled it up with cold water and positioned himself alongside the door, getting ready to make entry. He waited until it sounded as if Lucas was about to climax, and then Mike breached the door. It flung open, and Mike saw Lucas's muscular, toned, dark-brown legs thrusting hard, and another set of legs, feet wearing desert boots, resting on Lucas's shoulders.

"What the fuck? Who is that?"

Mike answers, "It's me, dick," and begins shooting Lucas in the ass with the Super Soaker. "I'm just checking in to see if you're ready for your enema."

"'Ey, fucker, stop it," Lucas shouted.

A feminine voice asks, "Me, Papi? You want me to stop?"

"No, Mami, you keep going; I'm almost finished. Mike, you stop it. It feels good, but stop it; you're gonna give me a complex."

Mike stops and stares, dumbfounded by Lucas's statement. He says, "Aight, man, hurry up. I have shit to do. I wanted to check in with you real quick." Mike shuts the door and heads to the trauma bays to steal the supplies he needs to restock his aid bag.

Ten minutes pass before Lucas comes out of the room with his female companion. He walks her to the back door of the aid station.

She pauses just outside of the doorway, turns around, grabs Lucas's groin, and pulls him toward her, slamming their bodies together. She leans in, and they exchange a long, passionate kiss. She pulls away, saying, "That's so you'll remember me, Papi. And just so you know, I am into sharing with friends." She looks past Lucas and stares at Mike, shooting him a wink and blowing him a kiss before turning to leave.

Lucas shut the door behind her and turned to Mike. "Damn, bro. You down for some tag team?"

Mike laughs. "Nah, man. Sounds like fun, but Vanessa doesn't like to share. Plus, I know where your dick has been. Anyways, man, I'm just here to steal supplies and check in to see if anything has happened around the AO with the other medics."

Lucas pauses for a minute, trying to recall the events of the past few weeks. "Carson and the boys from Bandog hit a few daisy-chain IEDs, but no one was hurt, and they didn't see anyone. Annihilators encountered a few small-arms ambushes. Took some minor injuries, but nothing serious. Demon Company had some sniper fire and a complex attack. No injuries, but it seems like haj was testing their response times. Other than that, not much shit has been going down."

"Thanks for the intel, man. Oh, I took some Kerlix, QuikClot, Ace wraps, some meds, and a few rolls of tape."

"No worries, man. I got you."

Mike grabs all his stuff and heads out.

"'Ey, Mike," Lucas calls out, "let me know if you change your mind about that little *chica* that was just here. I know you know she's bad."

Mike chuckled. "Thanks for the offer, dude, but I'm good." Mike turns to walk away, throwing a peace sign over his head with his right hand.

Mike finally made it back to his hooch. Opening the door of the room, Mike felt the rush of cold air chilling his skin. As the door opened, the outside light shone through the room, illuminating the picture of Mike and his family he had taped up on the wall. Bringing two fingers to his lips, he kissed them and threw the kiss to the picture. He dropped his gear to the floor, walked over to the mini fridge in the corner of the room, and grabbed a Rip It and a cold bottle of water.

After downing the Rip It and water, Mike situated his gear, gathered his shower stuff, and made his way to the shower trailer. The cold water felt good on his body. Now that he was back on the FOB, a million thoughts ran through his head. Mike started thinking about Vanessa. He thought about how, when he got home, he would pull her close, kiss her lips, and nibble her neck. Then run his hands along the side of her body, from her hips up. Then take her hands, raise them over her head, and cross her arms at the wrists. Then lean in and bite her softly on her bottom lip.

Mike noticed himself getting erect as he continued to think about returning to Vanessa. His mental fantasy continued, and Mike started to grip and rub his hard member. Mike envisioned Vanessa biting her lower lip, her eyes rolling back, and her body quivering the same way she did when she climaxed from pleasure. Mike placed his left hand on the shower wall to keep himself from falling as his knees weakened, and he let out a soft grunt.

"Hey, Mike!" a voice called out. "You in here?"

Mike snapped back to reality. "Yeah, J, what's up?"

"Oh nothing. I just saw your stuff was back, and I wanted to see if you wanted to go to chow."

"Yeah, man, give me a few."

"Aight, man. Well, I'll wait for you in the room."

Mike finished rinsing off, changed, and headed back to the room.

After chow, Mike returned to his room and turned on his laptop to check his emails. Mike knew he had some time before Sergeant Miller came to the room for some Guitar Hero. As his email pulled up, he saw an email from Em. His heart skipped a beat, and his chest tightened.

Why is she emailing me? What could this be about? Mike thought to himself. He quickly clicked on the email and started reading.

My Dearest Mike,

I know it has been a long time since we last saw each other. But the memory of our time together has never strayed far from the forefront of my mind. I have waited for so long for that to happen. I cannot tell you how many nights I have dreamed of me being in your arms. Feeling your body close to mine. Falling asleep hearing your heartbeat.

I often find myself thinking about you and dreaming of the life we could have had. Although, I know that the moon and stars have not aligned yet.

A lot has been on my mind the past few months. Not just us, but now there is even more to consider. The weight of what I am about to say will have monumental consequences that will impact more than just us. And you being where you are now and doing what you're doing, I really contemplated whether or not I should tell you what I am about to tell you.

The night we met was the best night of my life, and it has given me a great gift. I felt sick the past few months and went to see my doctor. It turns out that I now carry a part of you in me. I am pregnant with your child.

I am not asking you for anything. I am not going to file for child support. I am not trying to break up your home. I just wanted you to know. I wanted you to know just in case you didn't make it back.

Please know that I love you. I am always thinking about you.

Love always,

Em

Mike was in shock. He read and reread Em's email. The world around Mike faded away. *She's pregnant! Oh my God.* A million thoughts ran through Mike's head.

A loud pounding on Mike's door snapped him back to the present.

"Doc! Doc! You ready? Open the door," Sergeant First Class Miller calls from outside Mike's room.

Mike gets up, makes his way to the door, and opens it up to see Sergeant First Class Miller standing at his doorstep in his basketball shorts and Alabama Crimson Tide football shirt. "Hey, Rich, now is not a good time. I got some news from back home that I need to go address," Mike stated.

"Everything okay, Doc?"

"Yeah, man. Just something I need to clear up. I'm good, though. Thank you for asking."

"Okay, Doc. Well, if you want to jam when you get back, just knock on my door."

Mike shuts the door and, in shock, sits in his room. He glances at his watch; it's 1645. Mike thinks to himself, *I have to wait fifteen more minutes before Em will be waking up in Texas.* He reads the email one more time before getting up and changing into his black PT shorts and grey Army T-shirt. After grabbing his radio, 9 mm Beretta, and a notepad with Em's number in it, he makes his way to the phone banks.

Mike picks up the phone and begins dialing Em's number. He takes a few deep breaths, trying to keep calm. Mike scrambles, thinking about what he is going to say.

The ringing stops, and Em picks up the phone. "Hello? Who is this?"

Mike freezes. A swell of emotions comes over Mike, but just hearing Em's voice puts him at ease.

"Hello, Em. It's Mike."

Em knew who it was as soon as she heard Mike's voice.

"How have you been?"

"I'm good, Mike. How are things over there? How are you doing?"

"I've been through worse. I, uh—"

Em interrupted, "You read my email, didn't you?"

"Yeah, I did."

"So what are your thoughts?"

"Um…I'm…ah…happy."

"It doesn't sound like it."

"It's complicated, Em. I mean, I'm excited, but it's complicated. In case you couldn't tell, I've loved you since the first day I laid eyes on you in the cafeteria at school. Your smile, laugh, and light drew me into your orbit, and I could never let go."

He could hear Em gasp at what he was saying, so he continued, "The night we spent together before I left was…was…the hardest night of my life. That night, you fell asleep in my arms. I stayed up watching you sleep. Seeing your face all busted up and feeling like I let you down killed me inside. You needed me, and I wasn't there. That feeling haunts me to this day.

"Now, with this. I…I…have that same feeling. Em, I'm married. I have kids with Vanessa, my wife. And although things aren't great between us, I can't leave her. I can't abandon my children. I owe it to them to be present for them—"

Em interrupts, "Mike, I'm not asking you to leave them. I'm not asking you to choose between me or them. I just wanted to tell you we are going to have a baby. We are going to be forever tied to one another. Mike, I have a great job. Great benefits. I make plenty of money to support me and our child. I want you to have the opportunity to be present in his life when you are ready."

"Goddammit, Mike, get it through your hard head that I love you. I love you even though I know deep down that we may never be together. But at least with this, with our child, I will at least have a part of you for myself. Some tangible part of you that will love me unconditionally. A piece of you that is mine and...and not something I have to share."

In the phone booth, Mike sat in silence after hearing what Em had to say. After a while, he said, "Em...I don't know what you want me to tell you. If things were different, if life was different, I would have a different response. But not now. I don't know what you expect me to say. I was going to ask if you were going to keep it, but it is obvious from how you are talking, and from how you grew up, that you are going to keep it."

Em gasped. "How the hell did that thought even cross your mind? Yes. Yes, I'm going to keep my child. Like I told you, I want nothing from you. I just wanted you to know. You know now. The rest is up to you. Be a part of our child's life...or don't. Look, I gotta get up and get ready for work. I'll talk to you later...or not. It's...whatever. Bye, Mike."

"Em...Em..." Mike calls out, but the deafening sound of the dial tone screams in Mike's ear. He hangs up and sits in the phone booth, lost and confused. He is paralyzed by the news and by how the conversation transpired. Mike picks up the phone receiver again and starts to dial.

The line rings until a man's voice answers, "Hello? Who is it?"

"Hey, old man. You got a sec to talk?"

"Oh hey, mijo. Yeah, I have some time. Is everything and everyone okay? You sound like something is bothering you," Tomas said.

Mike thought to himself, *It is amazing how my dad can tell something is wrong by the sound of my voice.*

"Yeah, Dad, things are good, and as far as I know, everyone is still alive. I haven't heard anything over the radio."

"Well, that's good to hear, mijo. So what's up? What's on your mind?"

Mike began crying.

"Hey, hey, mijo. What's wrong? What happened? Whatever it is, I'm sure it's not that bad."

"Dad... I fucked up, Dad. I fucked up," Mike said, sobbing.

"Hey, hey, son. Take a breath, and just tell me what happened."

"I got Em pregnant," Mike managed to say.

"Whoa. Wait. What? When did that happen?"

"Before I left, I had a training course I needed to do in San Antonio before I deployed. She was in San Antonio for a conference and saw a post I made on Facebook. She messaged me, and we met up. Next thing you know, we are at a club, dancing and having a good time. I didn't want the night to end, so we went back to her hotel room. And then…one thing led to another," explained Mike.

"Whoa. Okay, so then y'all met up again?"

"No, it was just that one time. The next morning, I got up, went back to my hotel room, and finished my training at Fort Sam," Mike explained. "Well, she emailed me a few days ago, but I didn't have a chance to check it until today; she told me she was pregnant. I just talked to her, and it ended badly."

Mike continued, "I don't know what to do. I feel like a piece of shit because, deep down, I want to be with Em. You know I've always loved her. No matter who I was with, I always came back to Em. No one could compare to Em."

"I know, son. I never understood why you and her never got together. I thought it might of happened that summer of your senior year. But you just up and left for the Army without saying anything to anyone. You always swore that you would never join the military, so I was confused when you did, and hurt that you didn't at least tell me. To this day, you still never told me why."

"Dad, it's best if you don't know. All you need to know is that she is part of the reason why I left. And when I left, I had to close off that part of me because holding on to hope that me and Em would be together was torture."

"Okay, son. What are you thinking?"

"I'm thinking that I really want Em to be in my life. I really want to be in my child's life.I'm thinking that this will be the end of me and Vanessa and that I will never see Logan, Jami, and Lexi. I'm also thinking that this may be the out I was looking for. Things between me and Vanessa haven't been good the past few years. She doesn't know it, but I know she cheated on me. I know that she is tired of me being gone. I know she is tired of being alone with three kids."

"Mijo, is that why you slept with Em? To get back at Vanessa because she cheated on you?"

"What?! No! Damn, Dad. I know I'm petty and an asshole. But not that petty. Plus, if that was the case, I would have done that when I found out. I'll admit I thought about it when I found out. But I couldn't blame her. I was drinking all the time, trying to numb the pain from my deployments. I was always in the field, training. I had angry outbursts and was just losing my shit. A woman can only take so much before she leaves.

"When I found out about her cheating, I decided I needed to change. I needed to get help. Not for her, but for me and the kids. My family means the world to me, and I was on the verge of losing them," Mike explained.

"I cut back on my drinking. We started going to marriage counseling and really tried to work on our relationship. But I felt like it was a little too late. I feel like she was checked out and is just staying until she has an opportunity to leave."

"I see. Well, son, what are you feeling?"

"I feel happy. Excited. Scared. I'm happy that I'm having a baby with the person I feel like I'm meant to be with. Excited at the possibility that this might be the chance for Em and me to be together. Scared that it will not happen. That, even though it looks like the moon and stars have aligned, it's still just not the right time."

An automated voice came on the line and said, "This phone card has five minutes left of talk time."

"Well, son, we have five minutes left, so I'm gonna make this quick. If the baby is the only reason that you are considering leaving Vanessa, then don't. You can still be a part of your child's life. I know you are worried about losing your family, but be honest and tell Vanessa.

If you are honest, hopefully, she can forgive you, like you did her. Marriage is hard work, and it takes both of you to make it work. Son, just remember that things work out as God intends for them to. Pray about it, and the answers will reveal themselves to you."

"Thanks, Dad. Sorry for bringing this drama into your life. Please don't tell Mom; that is the last thing I need right now."

"Anytime, son. And don't worry; I won't tell your mom."

Mike hangs up the phone, takes a deep breath, and exits the phone booth. He does a quick check to make sure he has all the items he came with, and then makes his way back to his hooch. On the way, he runs into Carson, who is coming from the DFAC.

"'Ey, dick," called out Carson.

Mike turns and gives Carson the middle finger. "Hey, fucknut. When did you get in?"

"A few minutes ago. I wanted to grab chow before they closed. Hey, man, you down for a drink?"

"Bro, after the conversation I just had, fuck yeah. I need a drink."

"Damn, man, that bad? Here or home?"

"Home."

"Aight, man. Give me a few minutes. Let me wash my balls and ass, and then I'll come over. We can sit on the roof and watch for fireworks."

"Okay, man, I'll see you in a bit."

About thirty minutes passed before Carson came and knocked on Mike's door. Mike grabbed his pack of cigarettes and an empty bottle for Carson to use for his dip spit. With everything gathered, they made their way to the tin roof of Mike's hooch and sat watching the night sky for tracer rounds.

"So what's up, man? What happened? Things good with the wife and kids? Do I need to tell Jess to go check on them?"

"Nah, man, they are good. You remember when we went to San Antonio?"

"Yeah."

"Well, let me tell you about that night we went out and I disappeared…"

Mike went on to tell Carson about Em and her being pregnant. He also told him about Vanessa's affair and how he was torn and didn't know what to do. They sat and talked about Mike's predicament for a while.

Then changed topics to Carson's homelife drama. Then their plans after this deployment.

This went on until three in the morning, when they called it a night.

Chapter 17

"You good over there, Doc?" Sergeant Marks asked over the tanks' intercom. Mike was lost in his own head, which was a dangerous place to be when out in sector. It had been three months since Em told him the news. Mike had done a lot of reflecting on the news, what he said, and how he acted.

Mike was still unsure what he was going to do. He didn't know how he was going to tell Vanessa, much less if he was even going to tell her. The only thing he did know was that he still loved Em. His love for Em, coupled with having a child together, made him question if his relationship with Vanessa was just an attempt to fill the void created by the night that had changed the whole trajectory of his life.

"Doc! Load a can round!" screams Sergeant Marks.

Mike is abruptly returned from his thoughts and finds himself right in the middle of an attack. Mike instinctively opens the turret door and loads a canister round. "Up!" Mike calls out over the intercom. The gut-punching pressure differential from the main gun's firing took Mike's breath away.

Over the intercom, Captain O'Neill relayed the developing situation back to the company headquarters, "Cobra Mike, Cobra Six. We are taking small-arms contact, approximately 15 pax. Vicinity grid, SR23557789. Engaging with coax and main gun. No damage at this time. Over."

"Cobra Six, Cobra Mike. Acknowledged all. Do you need additional assets or air support?" a voice over the radio asked.

"Cobra Mike, Cobra Six. That's a negative at this time. Spin up Gold and Green Platoon to do a post-battle damage assessment. And clean up any sleepers. Over."

"Cobra Six, cobra Mike. That's a good copy. Over."

Mike popped up out of the loader's hatch of the tank and started scanning his sector for any enemy reinforcements. Things were eerily quiet after the brief skirmish.

About twenty-five meters away, Mike saw movement down the alleyway he was watching.

Mike's hands clenched the handles of the M240 fully automatic machine gun. His thumbs were poised to depress the butterfly trigger, bringing the slumbering beast alive. "Possible enemy movement, twenty-five meters, at nine o'clock," Mike calls out on the intercom.

"Aight, Doc. If you see hostile movement, light them bitches up," Captain O'Neill responded.

Mike mumbles to himself, "Don't you do it, fucker. Don't fucking do it." Mike watches closely, waiting. Seconds drag on for an eternity. A glint of light catches Mike's eye, and he breaks his focus from the man halfway down the alleyway. A quick glance to the third floor of the building above where that man was standing, Mike sees a small handheld mirror. He returns his gaze to the man on the ground and sees him taking aim with a rocket-propelled grenade.

"RPG! Nine o'clock!" Mike screams out as he opens fire with the M240. The machine gun comes alive as Mike depresses the trigger. Mike stays steady and focused as he stares down the RPG hurling straight at his position.

Mike feels a hard tug on his pant leg as he falls backwards into the turret.

"Doc, get down," Captain O'Neill said over the intercom. "The fuck, Doc. You trying to get yourself killed?" No sooner than Captain O'Neill uttered these words, the tank shook from the RPG exploding on the side of the tank.

Sergeant Marks turns his turret down the alley and starts firing the coax gun. With surgical precision, Sergeant Marks was able to eliminate both enemy combatants. "Good eye, Doc. I finished them off for you," Sergeant Marks shouted into the intercom.

"Hey, guys," Private First Class Debois called out over the intercom, "you guys think this is gonna last much longer? I'm hungry."

Captain O'Neill quickly answered, "Didn't you eat before we left?"

"Yeah, sir, but I'm bulking right now, so I need to eat every three hours."

Sergeant Marks quickly interjected, "'Ey, D, you're always bulking, man. That's why you can barely pass tape."

Private First Class Debois got quiet for a second, then responded, "Damn, Sarge, why you gotta go there? We all can't be little hulks like you."

"What the fuck is that, a short joke? I'll fuck you up, Private," responded Sergeant Marks.

"Now, children, settle down. In case you guys forgot, we are still engaging bad guys," Captain O'Neill stated.

He was right. Two city blocks down, Staff Sergeant Hut was still taking fire.

"Cobra Six, Green One. Green element, four mikes out," First Lieutenant Frazier informs the group.

"Cobra Six, Gold One. We are right behind the Green element with twenty-five dismounts," First Lieutenant Salazar calls over the radio.

"This is Cobra Six. Acknowledge all. Green, I want you to fall back and let Gold push through and draw any fire from whoever is left. Break. Gold, sweep the streets till you hit Route Red Leg. Break. Once secure, drop your dismounts, establish a cordon, and search the green house at your three o'clock. Three insurgents ran into it. How copy? Over."

"Gold One acknowledged," said Lieutenant Salazar.

"Roger that, sir," said Lieutenant Frazier.

Mike watched as the movement of armored vehicles and soldiers masterfully conducted a symphony of coordinated death and destruction. He listened intently as the dismounts stacked and breached the house. Mike could hear the excitement in the squad of infantrymen going from room to room and from floor to floor as they searched the house. Mike could feel his heart race with each radio transmission from the soldiers.

After about seven minutes, First Lieutenant Salazar came over the radio, "Cobra Six, Gold One. Two houses secure, four enemy KIA. Holding the buildings and setting up security. Over."

Captain O'Neill responded, "Roger that, Gold One. Red Platoon is on their way out to provide overwatch. Should be there in about fifteen mikes. Break."

"Cobra Mike, Cobra Six. When Red Platoon is five mikes out, we will do a rolling tag-out and RTB. If we stay any longer, we'll need to be towed out."

"Cobra Six, Cobra Mike. Roger."

Making their way back to base, Red Platoon's tanks and crew pass by the Headquarters element. Mike sees Specialist Timmens, his medic, standing in the loader's hatch. Mike gives him the middle finger and then motions with his hand, simulating jacking off.

Specialist Timmens shakes his head and gives back the one-finger salute.

Turning his attention back to scanning his sector, Mike felt the hot air blow across his face.

"Doc, what the fuck happened back there?" asked Captain O'Neill.

Mike turned, looked at Captain O'Neill, and asked, "What was what?"

Captain O'Neill answered, "The attack started from your side. When I looked over, you appeared lost. That's not like you. Normally, you're on top of that shit."

Mike felt a wave of shame come over him. Captain O'Neill was right; normally he would have been more attentive to what was going on around him. But not today; today he was a million miles away. His mind was focused on Em and the whirlwind of drama that would ensue.

"Sir, I wasn't in it today. I just overlooked the threat. It won't happen again," answered Mike.

"Shit happens, Doc. No one died today. Get your head back in the game. Take the next two days off, and take care of the things you need to take care of. I can't afford to have my best doc not mission ready."

The brief firefight that just occurred gave Mike some perspective. *Damn that was close. It could have gone way different. I need to get my head in the game.* Mike rode the rest of the way in silence, just thinking about what transpired and reflecting on Em's news.

Upon returning to the FOB, Mike quickly helped the tank crew refuel and refit with ammo and prepped the tank in case it had to roll out again. He then quickly made his way to his hooch and changed into his PT uniform. After that, Mike jogged to the phone booths and started dialing Em's number. *C'mon. C'mon. C'mon, pick up. Pick up.*

"Hello?" Em answered.

"Em, it's me. Look, don't hang up. Please don't hang up," Mike said in a rush.

Em could hear the sense of urgency in Mike's voice.

"Look, I know it's super early, and I'm sorry. But I have to tell you this. I know the last time we talked I was an asshole. I was self-centered and…and…and just a complete fucking idiot. Over the past few months, I've done some thinking. And I've come to the conclusion that I want to be in your life and that of our child. If you'll have me—"

"Mike—" Em interrupted.

"No, let me finish. Em, I love you. You know that. I know that I'm married, but things between me and Vanessa are hitting rock bottom. I've known she wasn't happy for a long time. She has been so unhappy with me and with how things are going that she ran into the arms of another man. I stayed to work through it, but I'm pretty sure it's too late. When we talked the other day, she told me that she has had enough and is considering getting a divorce when I get back.

"Why try to force something that is not meant to be? Maybe this is our opportunity to be together. Maybe the moon and stars will finally align. I hope that you will give me the opportunity to be yours."

A deafening silence echoes through the phone line. Mike could hear Em breathing softly and fighting back tears. "Em, are you going to say something?"

Em clears her throat and begins, "Mike...I...uh... um...I'm not pregnant anymore. I had a miscarriage three weeks ago. I'm sorry you are going through that with your wife. But that's none of my business. You should focus on you and your family. Please don't call me again."

The phone lines goes dead, and Mike is left holding the receiver to his ear. A blank stare is fixed on his face. In a daze, he walks over to Carson's room and knocks on the door.

Carson opens the door to see Mike standing there, dazed, hurt, numb, dead inside, tears flowing from his eyes. Carson grabs Mike and helps him up the stairs. He gives Mike a big, brotherly hug, brings him into the room, and pours two glasses of bootleg whiskey.

"I'm here when you're ready, brother," Carson tells Mike.

Mike looks directly into his eyes, and they just sit in silence.

Chapter 18

The soft glow from the vital signs monitor illuminates Mike's face. The heart-rate line starts beeping faster and faster, followed by the sounds of the ventilator. Mike struggles to move his wrists, but can't; they are pinned to his sides. He begins thrashing his legs, kicking them up and down and side to side. He tries screaming, but nothing comes out. An overwhelming fear settles over him.

Where the fuck am I? I can't fucking breathe. Why can't I move my arms? Why can't I see?! Mike thinks as he tries to free himself. He screams in pain and frustration, but nothing is heard. Finally, Mike is able to break his left hand free and grab the item he felt rammed down his throat. With a swift, hard pull, he yanks out the ventilator tube.

At the same time, Mike hears a voice say, "Mr. Perez. Mr. Perez, please stop; you are in a hospital. Don't pull out your lines."

Mike did not hear the voice trying to calm him down and reorient him to the present.

Mike quickly undoes his restraints and kicks the nurses rushing in to subdue him. He feels his face and tears off the tape holding his eyelids shut.

Overhead, Mike hears, "Code grey, room 127. Code grey, room 127."

He manages to get on his feet; the cold floor shocks his senses. He staggers to the door of his room. He tries to run, but stumbles and falls to his knees. Mike rapidly scrambles back to his feet. His surroundings start to become clearer, and he slowly realizes where he is.

Mike manages to exit his room and make his way past the nurses' station, leaving a trail of broken medical equipment and shocked staff members.

This doesn't make sense, he thinks to himself. *What the fuck happened?*

A few hospital-staff members step in front of Mike, trying to redirect him and corner him, to calm him down and get him back to his room. Mike, however, is operating purely on survival instincts, his training, and his will to live. One of the hospital staff lunges at Mike. Mike swiftly dodges the man's attack and uses the staff member's momentum to slam him face-first into the wall.

Mike expeditiously evades the other hospital member. He then makes a break for the stairwell. As he reaches for the handle of the door, Mike feels his feet come out from under him. And a sudden pain in his left side. He sees the door go from being upright to horizontal. Mike can't breathe; there's a crushing weight on his chest.

"Don't move. Stop fighting. Mr. Perez, we are trying to help you." A heavily muscled security guard tackles Mike to the ground and uses his body weight to pin him down.

Mike struggles and maneuvers himself into position to mount a ground attack. He manages to create enough space to put the guard in an arm bar.

Just then, two more security guards rush over and pounce on Mike. He now has one security guard on each arm and another lying across his thighs.

Mike tries to thrash his arms and kick his legs. He screams, "Not today, haj. You're not gonna cut my fucking head off." He writhes in pain and fear, and lets out a primal scream, "Aaaaaaahhhhhhaaaa!!!!" Fear flows from Mike's face, and he starts crying. He continues to try to free himself.

The nursing staff rushes to Mike and administers a sedative.

Mike fights it. He fights to keep his consciousness. He can't move. His senses numb. The last thing he feels is the weight on top of him and the coldness on his back.

Mike fights to keep his eyes open. He sees Em standing over him with a shocked expression. Mike tries to reach for her, but can't because his arms are pinned. "Em...help me...please!" Mike cries out. "Help me..."

Em sweetly says, "Mike, calm down, my love. It will be okay. I'm here."

Mike finally submits to the chemicals injected into him, and he passes out.

* * *

Mike wakes up screaming, "NNNOOOO!!!!! Sully!!" He hears a fast beeping sound that matches his heartbeat. He is wet from the sweat oozing from his pores. He tries to wipe his head, but is met with resistance. A loud thud is heard as he struggles to move his arm. The bed starts to shake as Mike struggles to free himself from whatever is preventing his movement.

"Mike, Mike...sweetie. Relax," a voice calls out from the dark corner of the room.

"Em?" Mike responds.

"Yes, my love. It's me. I'm here." Em emerges from the shadows and moves to Mike's bedside. She takes his hand and leans in to give him a kiss.

Mike tries to hug her and again is met with resistance from the straps pinning his arms to the bed. He struggles to free himself. He fights to hold Em. He longs to hold her. He dreamt of having her close and having his lips interlocked with hers.

Em pulls away and gently caresses Mike's face with her right hand. She sits on his bed and leans close to Mike and says, "Mike, calm down. It's okay. Don't fight it. You are safe. You're back in Texas. Don't worry. Everything will be okay."

"Am I dreaming? Are you really here?"

"Yes, Mike, you are dreaming. This is just a dream. Soon, you'll be back asleep, and I will be gone. But you will still be here in the hospital."

"What happened? How did I get here?"

"I don't know. Shh"—Em took a rag and started to dry Mike's forehead and face—"relax, my love. Get some rest. You will need it; you have a long road ahead of you." Em kisses Mike on the forehead and slides in bed next to him, on his left side. She crumples the rag and sets it on the bedside table.

Mike soaks in the feeling of having Em close to him again. He pictures himself holding her and falling asleep together. Looking out the window, he sees a familiar skyline light up the night sky.

Mike thinks to himself, *If this is a dream, I don't want to wake up*, as he drifts off to sleep.

Chapter 19

Mike awakes and sees Vanessa sleeping at his bedside. He looks down at his arm; it's still tied to the bed. Mike moves slightly, trying to adjust himself. His movements cause Vanessa to stir and awaken.

Vanessa lifts her head up and sees Mike staring at her. "Oh my God. Mike, you're awake!" she states as she starts crying.

Mike continues to look down at Vanessa. "Good morning, my love. Did you sleep well?" asks Mike.

Vanessa cries harder and says, "They called me last night to tell me you woke up, and I couldn't believe it. I rushed over as soon as I got off the phone with the nurse. When I got here, they told me what happened. How are you feeling? Are you hurt?"

Mike vaguely remembered what she was talking about. He adjusted his position and felt a sharp pain in his side. His body ached as he moved around in bed. "Why am I tied up? What happened? Why am I here? What the fuck is going on?" a confused Mike asked.

"Baby, you were injured during your deployment. Chris was there when it happened, and he called me as soon as he could. He couldn't tell me much before the phones cut out. The Army told me that a mortar round exploded close to you, and you took most of the blast. Someone from the Army came by and left a card with a number for me to call once you wake up. They want to give you an award for what you did that day," explained Vanessa as she pointed to the bedside table.

Mike looked in the direction Vanessa was pointing and saw the card next to a crumpled-up rag.

Vanessa squeezes Mike's hand and kisses it over and over again, saying, "My God, Mike. I can't believe you're here. I can't believe you're awake. Let me call the nurse to untie you." She gets up to find a nurse.

Mike returns his gaze to the rag on the bedside table. *Was Em really here?* Mike thinks to himself. He looks out his hospital window and sees the Towers of America looming over Downtown San Antonio.

Fuck! What the hell happened? Mike tries to remember anything from his deployment, but all he sees is a dark void of nothingness. He concentrates harder, but there's only a blank slate, and his inability to remember makes him angry. *Why can't I remember? Why can't I see what happened to me?* he screams in his head.

Mike closes his eyes tighter and tries one last time. He controls his breathing and attempts to calm himself. Then a memory slowly creeps in, and he grabs it. Focuses on it. The image of a phone booth appears; he remembers feeling dead inside. *"Please don't call me again, Mike"* rings in his ears. Mike snaps his eyes open as a nurse and Vanessa, followed by a doctor, enter the room.

"Good afternoon, Mike. I'm Dr. Ferguson. Can you tell me where you are?" asked a woman in scrubs and a white coat.

Mike looks out the window again and then at the wall behind the doctor and nurse. He sees a sign that says, "Welcome to Brooke Army Medical Center."

"By the sign behind you, I'm guessing that I'm back in San Antonio."

The doctor and nurse look at each other in sheepish embarrassment. "Okay, bud, can you tell me who's the president?" asked the male nurse.

"Mickey Mouse," said Mike with confidence.

"No, sir. Do you know who the president is?" asked the nurse again.

A thin smirk came across Mike's face. Vanessa catches Mike's smirk and shakes her head. Mike answered, "Well, I voted for Mickey Mouse. But he didn't win, so it's still President Obama."

The doctor giggled and answered, "Good, you have a sense of humor. That should help with your recovery. I'm gonna do a quick exam and answer any questions you might have about your medical condition. Any questions you have about what happened downrange will have to be answered by your rear detachment commander. Do you have any questions before I begin?"

Mike shakes his head then pauses before asking, "I just have one question, Doc. How did I get here? And what happened to Chris and the boys?"

Dr. Ferguson looks at Mike and says, "Mr. Perez, I can't answer that. You will have to ask your chain of command. Okay?"

Mike nods his head in agreement and says, "Okay, Doc. What's the damage then? Why can't I remember anything?"

Dr. Ferguson begins to explain to Mike and Vanessa the extent of his injuries. She tells them that Mike has a long road to recovery and that he may never fully recover. Dr. Ferguson goes on to say that Mike had shrapnel throughout his body; the force of the blast blew him into the side of the armored vehicle, causing head trauma.

Mike and Vanessa sit in silence as Dr. Ferguson explains in detail the injuries he sustained. All the while, Mike stares at Dr. Ferguson with a blank expression on his face. He desperately tries to understand what she is saying, but none of it is making sense.

Mike looks at Vanessa and says, "Babe, can you get me the pencil? I'm thirsty."

Vanessa replies confusedly, "Pencil? Do you mean a glass of water?"

Mike gets angry and asks again, louder, "Yes, babe, I want the pencil to drink. I am thirsty. Now give me the fucking pencil!"

Vanessa scrambles to get Mike a glass of water.

Dr. Ferguson interjects, "Mr. Perez, please calm down. Outbursts like that will not be tolerated. This is also one of the residual effects from the blast. It's called aphasia. Mr. Perez might confuse words with other words. And he may have difficulty understanding things that are written or spoken. As I said before, you have a long road ahead. It will require a lot of work from both of you."

Vanessa looked at Mike and said, "I made a vow—in sickness and in health. I will stick by it."

Mike looked at Vanessa and smiled. Then he turned to Dr. Ferguson and asked confusedly, "Where are the boys, Doc? I need to get back to my guys. Where is my weapon? Where is Chris? Where's Carson?"

The nurse makes his way to the bed and unties Mike's hands. He explains to Mike that if he starts getting combative, the restraints will be put back on.

Mike nods his head in acknowledgment. Once his hands are free, he holds Vanessa and starts crying. Mike still is unsure of what is going on; he just knows he is happy to see Vanessa. He turns to her and asks, "Where are the kids? How are they? What happened to me? How did I get here?"

Vanessa pulls back slightly from Mike's embrace, looks him in the eyes, and answers, "The kids are fine. They are with your parents. They are scared, but they are strong. They will be okay. As for the guys, I don't have any answers. They were extended for six months, and that was three months ago. That's all I know. We will need to call the guy that gave me the card. He can explain everything. But, first, I need you to focus on getting better."

Mike's face turns red as he starts to get angry. He can feel himself get mad, and he tries to calm down by focusing on slowing down his breathing. "No, Vanessa,

I need to know how my guys are doing. They need to know I'm alive. I need to know *they* are alive. Call the number on the card," Mike states through gritted teeth.

Seeing Mike get that angry scared Vanessa. She had seen him mad before, but nothing like this. She could see it in his eyes; something was different. He was different. He looked cold and dead inside.

Vanessa swiftly picks up the card and takes out her cell phone. Audible beeps are heard as she dials the number on the card and says, "Hello, this is Vanessa Perez, Staff Sergeant Perez's wife. I am calling because he is awake now and is asking to see y'all... Okay... Uh-huh... Tomorrow. Okay. I'll let him know. Thank you. Goodbye." Vanessa turns to Mike and lets him know that someone from the unit will come to visit tomorrow.

"That's good," Mike says as he lies back. Mike slides over to one side of the bed and motions for Vanessa to lie next to him.

Vanessa climbs into bed and nestles close. She is careful to avoid lying on any of his bandages.

They spent the rest of the afternoon talking and catching up. She filled Mike in on what she could about his injuries and what the other wives from the unit told her about the guys. Eventually, exhausted, Vanessa fell asleep holding him.

Mike kisses her softly on the top of her head and whispers, "I love you, *mi amor*." Out of the corner of his eye, he catches a glimpse of the crumpled-up rag on his nightstand…

Was it a dream, or was Em really here?

Chapter 20

Mike lay looking out the window as the sun came up over the skyline. The pinks, oranges, purples, and light blues swirled in the sky with splashes of light-grey clouds; they all combined to paint a beautiful scene. Mike fixated on the sky and thought that this picturesque sunrise reminded him of the mornings he sat on rooftops in Iraq.

A cascade of thoughts and emotions overcomes Mike. Tears start to flow from his eyes. First, one at a time, but then they give way to a floodgate of runaway tears. Mike tries to muffle his sobbing so as to not wake Vanessa, who is curled up in the corner of the room.

Vanessa's motherly instincts force her to wake up at the sound of crying. She sees Mike in his vulnerable state and rushes over to him. "Baby, what's wrong? Are you in pain? Can I get you something? What do you need me to do?" asks Vanessa. She grabs Mike and holds him tightly.

Mike buries his face in Vanessa's chest and begins to violently cry. "What the fuck is wrong with me? I need to go back! I need to be with my guys! I'm fine! Let me fucking go!" shouts Mike.

Vanessa is lost. Hurt. She wants to help Mike, but doesn't know how. She clasps Mike's head between her hands and positions his head so that she can look him in the eye as she says, "Mike, my love. Look at me. The guys are okay. You are okay. I need you to be here with me. I need you to get better. Once you're healed, then you can get back to your men. Please, please calm down."

Mike slowly begins to settle down. He looks at Vanessa and says, "No, you don't understand. I need to be there for them. I have to make sure they come home safe. I can't lead them from here. Who's gonna look after them?"

"Mike, look at me. You will be healed and back to training and leading your men. Later today, Master Sergeant Malone and Captain Riordan will be by to give you an update on your unit. They are leaving Fort Hood around eight o'clock," stated Vanessa.

Mike glances at the clock to look at the time; it reads 0630. He thinks to himself, *Two hours. This will be the longest two hours of my life.* Mike lifts up his arms to adjust himself in bed and catches a whiff of himself. His face scrunches, and he gags slightly. "When was the last time I showered?" asks Mike. "My pits smell like a mole's butthole." Then he lifts the blanket covering his legs and wafts the air surrounding his crotch. He gags and states, "Oh God, my balls smell like a dumpster full of shit. Can I take a shower?"

Vanessa chuckles slightly and says, "I'll ask the nurse when they come in to report."

Mike's face reddens, and he starts shouting, "No, I want to fucking shower. I smell like fucking dick cheese. I need a shower. What the fuck?! Why is it so damn difficult to do simple shit!"

Mike's outburst upsets Vanessa. "Mike, please calm down. Fine, I'll go ask now. Give me a second," says Vanessa. As she gets up from Mike's bedside, she starts to cry.

A nurse is drawn to Mike's room after hearing his shouting. Vanessa meets the nurse at the doorway, and they walk into the hall, out of Mike's earshot.

A few minutes pass, and Mike grows impatient. Mike mumbles, "Man, fuck this. All I want is a simple fucking shower and a shave. I don't need to ask for fucking permission. I'm a grown-ass man." He begins pulling out his IV lines and taking off his compression boots.

Mike throws his blankets off, turns his feet sideways, and lets his feet touch the ground. He can feel the cold, hard floor through his nonslip socks. He edges his way to the side of the bed and tries to stand, pushing himself up and distributing his weight on his feet. His legs are wobbly as he tries to take a step.

Mike manages to take one step before falling face-first on the ground. His head hits the windowsill and then bounces off the floor. A golf-ball-sized knot quickly develops on his forehead, along with a gash. "Mother fuck! Goddamn fucking son of a bitch! Fucking son of a cunt fucking douchebag tomfuckery!" Mike shouts out in pain and frustration.

Vanessa and the nurse rush back into the room, only to find Mike struggling to get to his feet.

Mike starts yelling again, "Leave me alone. I can do it. I don't need help." Tears start flowing as he continues, "I can do it myself." Mike manages to get to his knees before stumbling forward again.

The nurse swoops in and grabs Mike before he can fall again.

Mike starts to flail his arms as if he were fighting an invisible person.

"Mr. Perez, please stop swinging your arms. You are going to fall if I can't get a better grip on you," the nurse says.

Vanessa screams, "Mike! Stop it. Stop it. If you don't settle down, they will have to sedate you and strap you down to the bed again."

Hearing Vanessa's words stunned Mike. He started to settle down.

The nurse was able to get Mike back into bed and say, "Mr. Perez, give me a few minutes to call the docs and let them know what happened. They will be by to evaluate you and talk to you about your treatment plan. I will also gather some things to get you showered and shaved. Please stay put." The nurse then exited the room.

A traumatized Vanessa sat quietly in the corner, rocking in her seat while clutching Mike's hoodie, which she wore when she missed him. A stream of tears flowed from her eyes. She was scared. This was not the Mike she knew. This was not the Mike she loved. A flood of thoughts started to run rampant in her mind.

Vanessa had seen Mike come back from a deployment in bad shape, but not like this. When he returned from his last deployment, the aftermath had taken a toll on their relationship. She knew that she could not go through that again. The drinking, angry outbursts, and paranoia scared her.

Vanessa saw Mike staring at her. She was paralyzed with fear; she did not want to move.

Mike saw the petrified look on Vanessa's face. A feeling of guilt and shame came over him. He knew that he shouldn't have yelled, and his behavior was unacceptable, but he could not control himself. He knew that his actions were not appropriate, but he did not know why he was acting this way.

"Vanessa...I'm..." Mike started, "um...I'm...sorry. I don't know what came over me. I—"

Vanessa interrupted, "Mike, don't. Just don't. I'm gonna take a walk; I need some air. I just need a few moments to settle down. The nurse will be in shortly to help you shower, and the guys from your unit will be by sometime after that. I'll be back for that. Just give me a moment."

Mike's somber expression overtook his face. All he could do was nod his head in acknowledgment and watch as Vanessa stood up from her chair and left the room.

After Vanessa leaves Mike's room, she pulls out her phone and dials a number.

A man's voice picks up on the other end. "Hello? Vanessa? I thought you weren't going to call me until everything was done. Is everything okay?"

Vanessa stands silently in the hospital corridor, listening to a voice she has not heard for some time.

The voice asked again, "Hello? Vanessa, you there?"

Chapter 21

Mike finishes his shower and, using the four-wheeled walker his day nurse brought him, slowly makes his way to the bed. As he passes the mirror, he catches his reflection out of the corner of his eye. Mike pauses and turns his head to get a better look at his war-torn and battered body.

The right side of his back was covered with hundreds of scars in various stages of healing. His once pristine back tattoo was now distorted and barely recognizable. But the thing he noticed most was the amount of muscle mass he'd lost. He remembered the last time he weighed himself before his injury; he was an extremely lean 225 pounds. Now, he looked as if he weighed 150 pounds.

A weight he had not seen since his high school wrestling days.

The man Mike saw in the mirror was not the same one he remembered. Mike knew the man in front of him had a familiar face, but the rest was unrecognizable. He felt as if he were a stranger in another person's body.

Vanessa stood outside Mike's hospital room, watching him try to reconcile who he saw in the mirror. She could see the distress and confusion on his face, and she empathized; this was the first time Mike had seen himself since he was injured. But she remembered when she first saw Mike after he was medevaced back to Texas. Since then, she'd been forced to watch the man she loved waste away.

"Hey, sexy cheeks, is it a little breezy back there?" asked Vanessa, staring at Mike's naked rear end protruding out of the back of the hospital gown. "You know, those pants are supposed to go on your legs, not your shoulders," continued Vanessa.

Mike smiled. "The first minute to look is free, but it's twenty bucks after that. But, for you, I'll waive my fees."

Vanessa walked into the room and was about to help Mike. She sensed his apprehension, though, and quickly changed directions and headed to the bedside chair.

Mike continued to slowly make his way to the bed and get settled in. "Vanessa...I am sorry. I don't know what's wrong. I just want to hurry up and get back to my guys. They need me. I didn't realize how much I've wasted away. I can barely walk. It hurts to move. It hurts to stay still. I just hurt, and I don't know why."

"Mike, I can only imagine how difficult it must be for you to need help. To ask for help. But I am your wife. I am supposed to be here with you through thick and thin. Better or worse. Health and sickness. Goddammit, Mike. Why can't you be here for me and the kids? You don't see them cry themselves to sleep every night when you are deployed. You don't have to explain to them why you can't go to their father-daughter or father-son day. You don't see me sleeping in your shirt and holding your hoodie to feel close to you."

Mike stared at Vanessa as she continued, "Goddammit, Mike, why did you do it? Why did you cheat on me with her? Why did you throw away everything we have built together? I hate you for what you've done. But after almost losing you, I realize that I love you, and I can't live without you. When you were in the coma, there were some times that your heart stopped, and we almost lost you. I couldn't take it."

Mike was shocked by what Vanessa was saying. He thought to himself, *How did she know? Did Em come here and tell her? Why would Em do that?*

But Mike's surprise soon turned to anger. He shot back, "What *I* did? *What I did?* I didn't do it maliciously. I'm not the one that ran into someone else's bed. I am not the one that had a full-on affair with someone. I had sex with Em. Once. One fucking time. Do I wish it wouldn't have happened? Yes. Yes, I wish that it didn't happen. But it did. But for a whole year—*a whole goddamn year*—you were fucking some dude and acting like it was nothing. And *you* want to lecture *me*? You can go fuck yourself with that nonsense."

Vanessa begins to cry as Mike continues, "When you asked me to marry you, I knew that I loved you and wanted to be with you. I was awestruck by you. And I felt it in my core that I wanted to be with you—"

A loud knock on the hospital room's door stops Mike. He can't finish telling Vanessa how he feels.

The door opens to reveal two men wearing pressed Army combat uniforms. One of them says, "Sergeant First Class Perez? Are you awake? It's Captain Riordan and Master Sergeant Malone."

"Uh, this is Staff Sergeant Perez's room, sir," answered Mike.

Captain Riordan and Master Sergeant Malone enter the room, holding a few green binders and little navy-blue boxes. "Nah there, Sergeant First Class Perez. According to the paperwork I have, you are out of regs, son. It clearly states that Staff Sergeant Michael Perez is promoted to Sergeant First Class." Captain Riordan leaned over the bed's rail and pinned on Mike's new rank.

Mike smiled uncomfortably and looked at Vanessa. She could see the fear in his eyes, so she leaned over to grab Mike's hand in comfort.

"Sergeant First Class Perez, we also want to present you, on behalf of a grateful nation, the Bronze Star with Valor and the Purple Heart. For your actions and wounds sustained in combat. Your dedication and selflessness saved the lives of fifteen fellow Stallion troopers," said Master Sergeant Malone. He handed the medals to Captain Riordan, who promptly pinned them on Mike's hospital gown.

"Um…thank you, Sir, Sergeant. But, uh, I don't deserve these medals. I was just doing my job. I was taking care of our boys so they could get home and see their families," Mike begins as he starts to rub the back of his head.

"Well, son, you did just that. The men you and Staff Sergeant Chris Williamson saved that day will be able to go home and see their loved ones," stated Captain Riordan.

Master Sergeant Malone interjected, "Doc, I've known you since you were a private. Since I've known you, you have always taken good care of us. Now, let us take care of you, Doc. Rest up. These medals are a token of the appreciation and gratitude the guys have for you."

Mike nods his head solemnly in acknowledgment.

Master Sergeant Malone could see that Mike was itching to ask something. "Doc, they are fine. Alpha Company took a few casualties from two VBIEDs. And Charlie Company had a few close calls out at the JSS. But they made it through okay. Right now, the unit should have just made it back to Kuwait; they are refitting until they get cleared to come home."

Mike's eyes swelled up with tears brought on by mixed emotions. Ultimately, he was glad that his men were safe and coming back home.

Captain Riordan and Master Sergeant Malone sat and talked with Mike and Vanessa for a few hours.

"Sir, you ready?" Master Sergeant Malone finally asks. "We are gonna need to get going if we want to beat traffic and get home at a decent time."

Captain Riordan and Master Sergeant Malone get up and say their goodbyes to Mike and Vanessa. She walks them to the door, then returns to Mike.

Mike stares sternly at Vanessa and says, "Vanessa, I knew all this time. And I still stayed. And I will continue to stay with you. I will not give up on us. But you have a decision to make. I fucked up. I own it. But it will never happen again. I will never see Em again."

"How about when you pick up your son for visitation? You will have to see her then, won't you?" asked Vanessa.

"What are you talking about? What son?"

"Don't act like you didn't know," said Vanessa.

Mike quickly recovered. "No, not if you don't want me to. I can try to arrange it where I don't see her when it is my time with my son."

"I don't know, Mike. I am going to need some time to think about this. Everything is still so fresh and raw. I need some time to think."

Mike nodded. Then, attempting to choke down his tears, he said, "Okay then. Take the time you need. If you stay, I promise you things will be better. *I* will be better. If you decide to leave, I am not going to stop you. I will respect your decision. Just know that I love you either way."

Vanessa silently gets up to leave. As she breaches the doorway, she turns to look at Mike and says, "I love you, Mike. I just don't know if I can come back from this. I don't know if *we* can come back from this." She turns and walks away.

In the atrium of the hospital, Vanessa takes out her cell phone and dials a number.

"Hello, Vanessa. Are you going to say something this time?" asks a man's voice on the other end of the phone.

"Do you have some time to talk?" responds Vanessa.

Chapter 22

Mike positions himself between two upright parallel bars. Looking toward the other end of the bars, Mike stares at Dave, his physical therapist.

"Aight, you crusty old man. I know you're faking. Get your ass down here, and show me what you got," said Dave.

Mike smirked at Dave, gave him the middle finger with his right hand, and said, "Fuck you, guy. Even in my broken state, I'll still whip your ass!" Then Mike began walking forward. He slowly and steadily moved one foot then the other, alternating bracing himself with one hand after the other.

"Keep it up, Mike. We will get you walking and back in the fight in no time."

Mike can feel his legs shaking, and he starts to give up. "Fuck! Fuck! Fuck!" he exclaims.

"Don't you do it, Mike. Don't quit. A few more steps. Three…two…one. Good job, Mike. Good job. That's enough for today. Let's get you back to your room to get some rest."

Mike is escorted back to his room by a staff nurse; he finds Vanessa sitting there, waiting for him. Mike's pulse quickens, and he gasps silently.

"All right, Sergeant First Class Perez, we are back in your room, and it appears you have a visitor. I'll get a quick set of vitals, and then I'll let you be," said the nurse, promptly attaching Mike to the vital signs machine.

Mike could feel Vanessa's eyes fixated on him. He did his best to act normal, but deep down he knew her being here could only go one of two ways. Mike regained his composure. He waited for the nurse to exit before he said, "It's been a while, babe."

"I know. And I see you've made some improvements while I've been gone," Vanessa said, pointing to Mike's beard. "I like it. It suits you."

Mike's lips curled up, and a glimmer of a smile flashed for a brief second before his face returned to its usual stoic expression. "It's good to see you. How have you been? How are the kids?"

"The kids are good. They ask about you all the time. But I think it's best if they wait to see you closer to the time you get out of here."

Mike nods his head in agreement and says, "Yeah, I think that's best. And you? How are you really doing?" Mike could tell by the serious look on her face that the conversation was going to get really intense very quickly.

Vanessa paused for a few moments before starting, "Mike, I've…the past few weeks, I've been doing a lot of thinking…"

Mike felt himself holding his breath and clenching his teeth in anticipation of what Vanessa was going to say.

"And I would be lying if I said I could forgive and forget what you did. What hurts the most about all of this is that you knew I wanted another child, and you were adamant about not having one—"

Interrupting, Mike said, "Vanessa, I didn't mean for that to happen."

"No, let me finish. I've thought a lot about us, and I prayed about what to do regarding your child. And what I've come to realize is that I *do* love you. I *do* want to be with you. We both made mistakes, and if you can promise me that you will be honest with me and not keep any secrets, I will do the same. We also have to go to marriage counseling. If you agree to this—"

Mike blurted out, "Yes. Of course. Anything you say." He motioned for Vanessa to come closer so he could hold and kiss her.

They held each other for a bit. Mike could still feel an uneasy tension in the air, but he felt hopeful. Deep down, however, he had a feeling something was going to go wrong. Way wrong.

Chapter 23

A few months pass...

Mike and Vanessa are sitting side by side in the hospital room, waiting for Captain Riordan and Master Sergeant Malone to visit again.

"They didn't tell you why they were coming?" asked Mike.

"No. All they said is that they were coming to see you at noon today."

Anxiously, Mike gets up, grabs his crutches, and starts pacing around the room.

Vanessa can see the amount of distress Mike is in and says, "The doctors said that you might be discharged from the hospital in a few weeks. I think that it might be a good time to bring the kids by. They have been asking about you a lot recently."

Mike stops pacing and looks intently at Vanessa, his eyes momentarily glazed over. Mike's blank facial expression scares Vanessa. It is as if he is physically present, but his mind is elsewhere. "Mike! Mike, did you hear me?"

Mike shakes his head and shoulders as if a cold chill has run down his spine; he turns his head toward Vanessa. "What? Did you say something? I'm sorry, baby. I must've spaced out. What did you say?"

"I said that since you will be discharged soon, I think I should bring the kids to see you," repeated Vanessa.

"I would love that. I have missed them something fierce."

"I've also talked to the chaplain. He gave me some good marriage counselors in the area for us to see when we get out of here."

Mike smiled and said, "That sounds good, babe. I am really glad that you have given me another chance. I promise that things will be better. *I* will be better."

Vanessa looks down and wonders if she is making the right decision. *Should I really give Mike another chance? Was it just a fling?*

"Babe, is everything all right?" asked Mike, sensing Vanessa's hesitancy.

"Yes, my love."

"You have to forgive me if I don't believe you."

"This is not something we can talk about. We both will have to work at this. I was wrong, and I own that. But if we both are committed to fixing our relationship, then we both will need to be honest with each other."

Mike uses the crutches to make his way to the chair beside Vanessa, and then he sits down. He takes her hand and looks deep into her eyes. "My love, I will do whatever it is I need to do to make it right." Mike leans in and kisses Vanessa softly on the forehead. As Mike's lips pull back from her forehead, there are three knocks on the door.

"Hello, am I interrupting?" asked Captain Riordan.

"No, sir, come on in," answered Mike.

Captain Riordan and Master Sergeant Malone enter the room holding a manila folder. Mike studies their faces and can tell their visit is not going to be like the last one, which ended with medals being pinned on his chest.

"Sergeant First Class Perez, this will take a bit. We have spoken with your medical team, and from their assessment, they do not think that you will be able to return to your full duties. We came with some paperwork that you will need to fill out so that we can get your paperwork in order to medically retire you from the Army."

The last phrase echoed in Mike's ears. *I am being discharged from the Army. I don't want to get out of the military. What am I going to do? How can this be? Why is this happening to me?*

"A grateful nation thanks you for your service," says Master Sergeant Malone as he extends his right hand.

Mike looked at the hand and shook it haphazardly. "Thank you, Sir, Sergeant, but is there any way I can fight this and try to stay in?"

"I'm afraid not, son," said Captain Riordan. "The docs think it would be beneficial for you and the service to medically retire you. I know we are losing a great noncommissioned officer. And I'm certain you will do great things in your future. It just won't be in the Army."

Captain Riordan pulled up a bedside table and started laying out the paperwork in front of Mike. He explained each document as Mike signed it. Mike was in a daze, and everything Captain Riordan was saying was going in one ear and out the other.

After about an hour of explaining the process and signing paperwork, Captain Riordan and Master Sergeant Malone said their goodbyes, leaving a distraught Mike and a jubilant Vanessa. Mike felt his whole world crushing down around him.

In stark contrast, Vanessa felt as if her world were starting anew. This was not what she'd hoped and prayed for, but she felt this was exactly what they needed. A fresh start. A new beginning in which they could focus on each other. She would no longer have to wonder if Mike was in danger when he was deployed. No more weeks away from her and the kids for field training.

"Mike, are you doing okay?" asked Vanessa.

Mike nodded. "I am fine. I mean, as fine as I can be after wasting the past twelve years of my life."

"It's not a waste. You are being retired. You still get all your benefits. And now you can be with me and the kids. Now you don't have to miss their school events, sports, and dance recitals."

The life she just described sounded like hell to Mike. Deep down, he knew he would never settle down to a calm, peaceful suburban life. Although he desperately wanted a life of being home with his family, seeing his children grow up and become young adults of their own, Mike knew that life was not for him.

"Well, you heard them, babe. We have three months to get everything ready. We need to be packed and ready to give up the house on post. I have to get all my gear and turn it in…"

"My love, don't worry about that. I will head back to start packing up and taking care of the things we need to do to leave. I'll call Mom and Dad and see if we can stay with them until we can get back on our feet."

She gathered up her things and gave Mike a long, passionate kiss. "I know it seems like the end of the world now, my love. But I have a feeling that it will be the best thing for us."

Vanessa exited the hospital room and headed to the Fisher house, where she was staying. She packed up all her things and loaded them into the car to make the long six-hour drive home. A rush of excitement came over her. She thought to herself, *This is it. We can finally be a family.*

* * *

Later that night…

A heartbroken Mike sits in his hospital recliner, looking out at the city skyline. There is a sudden knock on the door. Mike looks at the reflection in the glass and asks, "What do you want? Why are you here? Haven't you done enough?"

Em fights back a swell of emotions and answers, "Can I come in? There are some things we need to talk about."

"Last I checked, this was a free country. Do what you want. And you're damn right; we have some things to talk about."

Chapter 24

Em enters the room and sits across from Mike. An uneasy silence fills the room. Em and Mike stare at each other until Em awkwardly turns her gaze to the floor.

Emotional complexities overcome Mike. "Are you going to say anything?" he asked.

"Where do you want me to begin?"

"How about you start with you lying to me about our son? That's a fucking good place to start!" shouted Mike.

Silent tears started to fall as Em began, "Mike, I'm sorry. The hardest thing I've ever had to do was lie to you.

I wanted to tell you, but I didn't want to be the reason you threw away your whole life. I couldn't be known as the other woman."

Mike's ears flushed as he interjected, "I told you we were done. I told you that I'd made up my mind; once I got back, we were going to get a divorce."

"And then what, Mike? Were we just supposed to start our lives on a lie? You lying to yourself that you didn't love Vanessa? Or that you wouldn't miss your kids after you two got divorced? And that this is the time we were meant to be together? A time that is rushed and forced?"

Mike stared deeply into Em's eyes. She could feel her heart flutter the way only he could affect her.

"Em, none of that changes the fact that you fucking lied to me about our son. I was devastated for you… for us…at the thought that you lost our child. I've gone through losing a child before, with Vanessa, and I saw how devastated she was. And here I was, thinking that you were going through that alone. I mean, fuck!"

Em buries her face in her hands and starts crying. "God-dammit, Mike. Stop being such an ass. Can't you see this is hard enough. I already feel like shit for lying to you. Can't you see that I'm scared. I'm scared that you may never want to see or talk to me again."

Mike turns his head toward the hospital room's door. He crosses his arms and sits in silence for a moment, then begins, "Em, what the fuck am I supposed to do? You lied to me. You betrayed my trust. I felt lost and hopeless. I wasn't planning to leave Vanessa just cuz you were pregnant. Shit really got that bad, to the point where we could not stand to be around each other. We pretended for the kids' sake, but that wouldn't have lasted long. But then you lied to me and told me that it wasn't meant to be. What the fuck was I supposed to do? And when I was blown up and needed someone, she was there. Not you."

Em tried choking down her tears as Mike continued, "Which is fucking crazy because in my lucid states, all I could think about was you. All I kept seeing was you. But you were only in my dreams. I kept seeing your face, feeling your touch, but it wasn't real."

Mike paused and looked away from Em. He gazed at the city's skyline then said in a low and serious voice, "When I was gone, I dreamt of you and the times we shared. But the thing that really gets me is that when I woke here, scared and alone, the person I saw, the person I knew could calm me was you. But you weren't here. I imagined you."

Em gasps and holds her breath. She shifts her eyes from the floor to Mike. "What?"

"I said, when I wanted and needed you the most, you were not here," repeated Mike.

"Mike, who do you think calmed you down after the security guards wrestled you to the floor? Who do you think wiped your head and tended to you when you were shackled to the bed? I did. I was the first one by your side when you made it back stateside. And I was the first one with you when you woke up!"

"What? How?"

"You know your dad is a man of his word. He kept your promise to contact me if anything ever happened to you. He didn't know that I had moved from Los Angeles back to Texas to take care of my mom."

A bewildered Mike sat staring at Em as she continued, "So when he called, I was already in San Antonio. I would come visit you every night. And stay as long as I could. The night you came out of your coma, I just happened to stop by. I hadn't seen you in a while because I respected Vanessa's wishes. But I had a feeling that I needed to see you that day."

Mike sat in silence, Em's words still echoing in his ears. He could not believe it. He thought, *She was here that night. I wasn't dreaming. So were the other times I felt her and heard her real too?*

"Mike, are you going to say something?"

Em's question made Mike think of the promise he'd made to Vanessa. "The moon and stars still have not aligned."

Em stared at Mike with an emotionless face. Her eyes began to well up. "I see."

"I made a commitment to Vanessa. We both agreed to give it another try. I do love her."

"More than me?"

"What? How can you ask that? She is the mother of my children and has been with me through some of my darkest times."

"I am the mother of your child too. I cannot make up for not being there in the past. You took that chance away from me when you left. But I'm here now."

Mike could feel his ears turning fiery hot as he remembered why he left so many years ago. "The fuck did you say? *I* robbed *you*? Do you even know why I left? Do you know why I'm here in the first fucking place? You knew I never wanted to join the military. You knew I hated the lifestyle and how hard it could be on families. So why do you think I did something I said I'd never do? It was because of you."

Em started to shake from fear and sadness. She recognized the man before her, but the person who was speaking to her was someone she'd never known. This was not the Mike she knew and loved. This was a soulless and heartless man. The dead eyes staring back at her sent chills down her spine as she sat quietly while Mike continued.

"Seeing the shape you were in when Ronnie left you, and thinking about all the unspeakable things he did to you, enraged me. Before I left your house I promised you everything was going to be all right. I was going to keep that promise. So I knew I had to do something. I saw him that night, and things happened that can never be undone. Because of it, I changed that night."

"What happened, Mike? What did you do?"

Mike shook his head and said, "It's best if you don't know. Leave it alone."

"That's bullshit, Mike. You can't say that and expect me to leave it alone while you pin your situation on me."

Mike noticed the slight taste of blood in his mouth. He realized that he was biting the inside of his cheek, trying to control his emotions. "Em, I can't do this right now. You can't be here. Please leave."

"Mike...please can I—"

"Em, get the fuck out!" shouted Mike, interrupting Em and pointing to the door.

A disheveled Em picked up her belongings and walked to the door. Before she exited the hospital room, Em stopped, turned toward Mike, and said, "Goodbye, my love." Then she left.

Chapter 25

A few days had passed since Mike spoke with Em. He had recovered enough from his injuries to be transferred from the hospital to the Fisher House, which was on the hospital's campus.

Over and over in his head, Mike replayed the conversations with Em. His actions and what he'd said to her weighed heavily on him. He knew deep down that Em was his soulmate, but Vanessa had been with him through some of his darkest times.

His thoughts are interrupted by the ringing of his cell phone. Mike grabs it and hits the button. "Hello?" he answers. "Oh hi, baby. Yeah, I'm doing good. I'm just here in my room, trying to relax. Oh, you are coming to see me with the kids?" Mike smiles and thinks to himself that seeing the kids should be a welcomed distraction. "Okay, baby. I'll see you then." Mike hangs up the phone and begins to clean up his room.

Mike hobbles to the kitchen counter where he has all his medications lined up. He opens a bottle filled with a narcotic for pain and swallows it with a swig from a day-old, half-empty beer bottle. Mike looks around his room and sees all the scattered alcohol bottles and fast-food wrappers. He thinks, *Fuck, I need to clean up.*

Grabbing a trash bag, Mike sets his arm on the counter and in a sweeping motion ushers all the trash into the garbage bag. Then he wanders aimlessly around the room, randomly picking up old pizza boxes and beer cans. Each time he bends over, Mike lets out a slight groan.

Fuck, I need to sit down, Mike thinks to himself as he walks over to the couch. He reaches for a freshly opened beer sitting on the coffee table and finishes it in one big gulp. His eyes get heavy as he stares at the wall, and he gently falls asleep.

Bang! Bang! Bang!

"Mike, are you in there?" a frustrated Vanessa shouts from the other side of the door. She tries to soothe a tired and hungry Lexi, and attempts to keep Logan and Jami calm as well.

"Mommy, is Daddy in there?" asked a concerned Logan.

"I don't know, mijo," answered a worried Vanessa.

Vanessa continued to forcefully knock on the door and shout, "Mike, are you there?" Her heart began to race, thinking about the worst-case scenario that could be on the other side of the door. She knew the dark places Mike could go after a normal deployment; she dared not imagine where he would go now.

Eventually, Vanessa heard movement on the other side of the door. Then a loud thud followed by an even louder, "Goddamn mother fucking fuck!"

After a few seconds, a disheveled Mike opens the door and is met with the joyous cries of "Daddy!" from all three of the kids. He bends down and hugs them, "Munchkins!" Mike looks up and sees Vanessa glaring at him. "Come in, guys. Let me show you around." Mike rushes Vanessa and the kids in. "Here is the kitchen, there is the couch with the TV, and over there is the bed and bathroom."

Vanessa critically scans the room and notices the three large trash bags. "I see you did some cleaning before we came," she proclaimed.

"What is that supposed to mean?" snapped Mike.

"Nothing. Do you have anything to drink? The kids are thirsty," Vanessa said as she walked toward the refrigerator.

Mike stopped her before she could open the refrigerator door. "No, I need to go shopping," said Mike, preventing Vanessa from seeing the refrigerator full of alcohol.

"Hey, kids, I have an idea. How would you like to go to the playground?" asked Mike.

The kids let out a loud and thunderous "Yeah!"

Mike helped Vanessa gather the kids and lead them to go to the playground. Once there, they had a good time sliding and chasing each other while Mike and Vanessa sat on a bench and watched.

"So were you able to get the house packed up?" asked Mike.

"Yeah," Vanessa answered coldly.

"What's wrong, Vanessa?"

"What have you been doing here?"

"What do you mean by that?"

"Has she been by?"

"No, babe. I told you that was over. We talked about it."

Vanessa shook her head and huffed. "How much have you been drinking?"

Mike glared at Vanessa and said, "What kind of a question is that?"

"You are going through a lot. You are recovering from your injuries. Here, pretty soon, you will be out of the Army. I mean, you just have a lot on you right now."

Bewildered, Mike looked at Vanessa. "Don't you mean *we*? *We* are going through a lot?" Mike started to raise his voice, but not loud enough to grab the attention of the kids. "I mean, *fuck*. I thought we agreed that we are going to work at this. This is gonna affect all of us."

"Mike, you know what I mean. I'm just worried about you. I'm worried for us."

Mike felt himself getting angry.

Vanessa saw the red flash in Mike's eyes, a look she had seen before. "Kids, let's go back home," called out Vanessa.

"Aw, Mom, we want to watch a movie with Dad," responded Logan.

"No, we need to go home and finish packing."

Mike looked at Vanessa and said, "Babe, they want to see a movie. Let's watch a movie."

Vanessa reluctantly agreed, gathered up the kids, and returned to Mike's room.

Mike sets up the TV for the kids to watch a movie. He makes his way to the kitchen counter and pops open a few bottles of pills, pours them into his hand, and throws them into his mouth. Mike then walks over to the fridge and tries to discreetly take a swig from a bottle of tequila.

Vanessa watches as Mike takes his pills and chases them with alcohol.

Mike turns and sees Vanessa's judgmental stare. He shakes it off, grabs a beer from the fridge, opens it, and takes a seat on a chair diagonal from the TV. The kids are sprawled on the floor, watching the movie.

Logan starts bumping into Jami.

"Stop," says Jami.

Logan pokes Jami in the shoulder.

"Bubba, stop it. That hurts," Jami says again.

"Boy, leave your sister alone," Mike says. He can feel himself getting agitated.

Logan then takes his foot and bumps it against Jami's foot.

"Logan, ssstttttooooopp!!!" calls out Jami.

Mike jumps up, throws his beer at the wall, and shouts, "Goddammit, boy. Stop it. Leave your sister alone. Fuck, why is it so damn hard for you to listen and behave!"

Logan turned ghost white and froze with fear. Jami and Lexi started crying.

Vanessa asked, "Mike, what the hell?"

"Why the fuck can't these kids listen? Is this the way you let them act while I was gone? They just do whatever the fuck they want? Fuck!" shouted Mike.

Vanessa gathered the kids in her arms and tried to console them. "Shh, babies. Dad is just upset right now." She rushed to get their stuff together and moved them toward the door.

"Mike, we are leaving. You need to calm down. They are just kids. They don't need to be around you when you are like this."

Mike gets up and makes his way to the bathroom. Without looking back, he says, "Fine, get out. I don't need you guys here now. Don't come back."

As Vanessa and the kids are leaving, Mike hears Logan ask, "Mommy, why is Dad so mad? I am sorry. I'll be better. I can behave. I don't want Daddy to hate me."

"No, mijo, he doesn't hate you. He is in pain. He doesn't mean it."

Mike, having heard all of this through the bathroom door, stares at his reflection in the mirror and starts crying. *Why did I overreact like that? The kids don't need to see that.*

A feeling of disgust came over Mike. A knot forming in his stomach, Mike clenched his fists and hit the mirror, shattering it into pieces. His knuckles started to bleed, so Mike exited the bathroom, walked to the kitchen, reached for his pills, opened the fridge, and grabbed a beer.

Fuck it, Mike thinks to himself. He swallows the rest of the pills in the bottle and chugs two beers. *Let's see how this turns out.*

Mike walks to the couch, sits down, and chugs another beer.

Chapter 26

Three loud knocks boom throughout the small Fisher House apartment.

Mike slowly opens his eyes and rubs his head. The banging is amplified in his hungover state. "Who the fuck is it?" shouts Mike as he stumbles out of bed.

The knocking continues and Mike yells again, "Hold on, for fuck's sake. Give me a fucking minute." He grabs a pair of basketball shorts lying at the foot of the bed and makes his way to the door. *Who the fuck is knocking this fucking early in the morning?* Walking past the kitchen counter, Mike stops to grab a handful of pills for his breakfast and washes them down with an open, day-old Monster energy drink.

The knocking intensifies as Mike gets to the door. He grabs the handle and opens it up saying, "Who the fuc—"

"Go ahead and finish that sentence, boy!" answered Tomas.

"Papi?!" said a confused Mike. "What are you doing here?"

"I was in town and thought I'd stop by. Your mom is with your *tia* shopping, so I figured I'd meet up with you and take you to lunch."

"Yeah, but you didn't call. What if I had been out?"

"I had a feeling you would be here."

"You're right. When you come to someone's house at the crack of dawn, it's a pretty safe bet that they will be home," retorted Mike.

"Son, it's eleven thirty in the morning."

Mike turns to look at the kitchen stove's clock, which is indeed showing eleven thirty-two. "Well, I'll be damn. Okay, Papi, let me shower real quick, and we'll go. Just make yourself at home."

Tomas scans the living room and notices the common theme of empty beer cans, liquor bottles, and energy drinks. He finds a spot on the couch and flips through the TV channels as he thinks, *I've never seen him like this before. I know he has been through some rough times, but never like this.*

Mike finishes his shower and exits the bathroom with a towel wrapped around his waist. Tomas catches a glimpse of his son, but barely recognizes him. His once muscular physique has been withered down by his injuries. Tomas sees the toll this war has left on his son's body, which carries visible scars left from the explosion.

Tomas could also see the mental toll Mike's injuries had taken from his son. He watched as Mike walked from the shower to the bedroom. Mike's once proud and upright walk now mirrored that of a defeated and broken man. *I wonder if I should tell him the news or not.*

Tomas shook his head, dismissing the thought, as he settled on the conclusion, *He needs to know.*

Mike shuts the bedroom door and starts to change. *Why is Dad here? Did Vanessa call him? He normally lets me know when he is coming to visit.* A million more thoughts enter his mind, but none of them is consistent with the news he is about to receive.

"So, Papi, where do you want to get breakfast?"

"Mijo, you mean lunch. The rest of us have already had breakfast...and second breakfast."

Laughing, Mike shakes his head. "Okay then, where do you want to have lunch?"

"Somewhere good. Somewhere that would remind me of home. I'm feeling a bit nostalgic."

"Ah, getting soft in your old age, I see."

Tomas chuckles and responds, "I may be old and soft, but I can still whip your crippled ass."

Mike stopped laughing and looked Tomas dead in the eyes. "Wow, that's low. You're gonna hit a man when he is already down?"

Tomas pauses and internally questions himself, *Did my last comment cross the line?* But then he catches a slight curl of Mike's upper lip. The same curl he always has right before he is about to deliver a smart-ass comment.

"Well, old man, other men have tried and failed. Plus, I've been blown up a few times, and I'm still here. So good luck with that. Anyways, I have this cane too, and I know how to use it against you young whippersnappers." Mike takes his cane and waves it in the air in a back-and-forth motion. "So try me."

They both laugh for a bit before Mike says, "You missing home, I have just the place for us to go."

Mike and Tomas walk to Mike's car, get in, and make their way to a restaurant that Mike goes to when he is missing his simpler life and reflecting back to when he was a kid visiting his grandparents in the Rio Grande Valley. This restaurant always reminds Mike of those family trips, more especially the ones to visit Tomas's dad.

On the last day of any trip to the Rio Grande Valley, before Mike and his family departed to return home, Tomas, Mike, Jose, and Mike's grandfather had breakfast at a little hole-in-the-wall Mexican restaurant that Mike's grandfather frequented. There, Mike drank in the sights, sounds, and smells of the local restaurant. He listened intently to the stories his grandfather and Tomas told because, at home, Tomas never talked much about his childhood. On the rare occasions that he did, it was only to tell the peaceful, calm parts, never his hell-raising adventures. However, when Mike's grandfather and Tomas got together over breakfast in that local Rio Grande restaurant, Mike heard about Tomas's more colorful and elusive past. Mike cherished those moments as they gave better insight into his dad's past.

On the car ride to the restaurant to which Mike is taking his father, Tomas and he engaged in their usual banter. The car was filled with joking and laughter. Mike enjoyed these moments for several reasons. He liked having quality time with his father, and Tomas understood Mike's dark sense of humor. Tomas also had a way of creating a space in which Mike felt he could say anything without fear of judgment or condemnation. But, most importantly, Mike could be himself without hearing a lecture about faith and prayer being the answer for everything.

Mike had a complicated view on faith and religion; it stemmed back to his childhood and was worsened after his first deployment. Mike questioned why, if God truly existed, He allowed to happen the things Mike had seen, experienced, and endured.

Tomas and Mike finally arrive at their destination. Getting out of the car, Tomas says aloud, "Cazadores. Huh, this is where you go when you are feeling homesick?"

"Yeah, they have great food. But, most importantly, they have the red Pizza Hut cups like they do in the Valley."

Tomas smiles and responds, "Well shit, then you know it must be good."

They enter the restaurant and sit in a back-corner booth. A young waitress comes by to greet them. "Hello, what would you like to order?" she says in broken English.

Because of the waitress's difficulty with English, Tomas started to order in Spanish; it translated to "Ah yes, is it too late to order breakfast?"

The waitress shook her head.

Tomas proceeded with, "I would like to have the barbacoa tacos with fried potatoes," again in Spanish.

The waitress nodded, turned to Mike, and asked with a big, flirtatious smile, "For you?"

"I'll have the same and some scrambled eggs and bacon."

"What do you want to drink?" asked the waitress.

Tomas answered, "A glass of orange juice and a water."

Mike replied, "Water and two cups of coffee."

As Tomas shoots an inquisitive look at Mike, the waitress repeats the order to Tomas and Mike and then leaves to place the order.

"Two cups of coffee?" asked Tomas.

"Yeah, well, you said you were feeling nostalgic, so one cup for me and the other for the memory of Grandpa."

Mike could see Tomas get a little emotional, but he seemed to quickly stifle those feelings as he said, "If that's the case, then you are going to need more sugar and creamer than that. You know your grandpa liked his coffee really sweet—sugar with a splash of coffee."

Mike smiles, then laughs, before answering, "Yeah, but who is going to drink that? And that would just be wasteful, so the spirit of Grandpa will just have to settle for straight black coffee. He can whip my ass later when we meet again soon."

"Soon?" repeated Tomas.

"Yeah. Well, I ain't getting any younger. I mean, you'll probably see him before I do. Seeing how you've been around since Texas was its own country. Remind me, which side did you fight on at the Alamo?"

Tomas let out a nervous laugh.

Mike could sense something was wrong. Usually, a comment like that would elicit a more robust laugh and a quick response. "Dad…what is it? What's wrong?"

Tomas's voice lowered, and the smile quickly faded.

The rapid change in Tomas's demeanor scared Mike.

Tomas's eyes began to tear up, and he struggled to speak.

"Dad…what is it?"

Tomas takes a big deep breath and manages to get out, "Mijo…they…uh…I have cancer."

The last few words echoed in Mike's ears. "What?" Mike managed to say. "Stop fucking with me."

Tomas could see the heartbreak on Mike's face. For Tomas, saying the words out loud made his diagnosis a real and overpowering force. For Mike, hearing those words shattered his whole existence.

A few moments of silence passed before, wiping tears from his eyes, Mike asked, "Does Mom know?"

Tomas shook his head and said, "You are the first person I've told. I don't think that she is ready to hear that. Plus, I don't think the church back home is fire-rated for all the candles she will light because of this."

Mike sniffles, dries his eye, and laughs. Tomas's comment had made Mike laugh, and that gave him hope. Laughing was a good release, and it gave Mike a sign that things might be okay.

Mike unloaded with a barrage of questions. "Do you know what kind? How far along is it? What's the treatment plan?"

"Hold on, son. I don't have all of the details. But it is still early. They don't think it's metastasized, but they think it is one of two types of cancer. One can be treated with chemo, and I will be cured. The other can be treated with chemo, but I will never be cured. It will always come back, and each time it does, it will come back more aggressively."

Mike sat there, intently listening to everything Tomas was saying. Everything felt surreal, as if he were in a bad dream and screaming, waiting to wake up.

The waitress came back with the food. Unsurprisingly, Mike had lost his appetite. He sat there and picked at his food.

The rest of the meal progressed in silence. Both men seemed to be reflecting on what had been said and internalizing the gravity of the situation.

Finally, Mike looked up at Tomas and asked, "When are you planning to tell Mom and Jose?"

Tomas looks up from his food and stares quizzically at Mike. "I don't know. Soon though. I've known about this for a few months now, and not telling anyone was eating at me."

Mike bites his lower lip in contemplation. "Well, when you do, let me know how it goes."

"I didn't want to tell you at first. But I knew I needed to. Vanessa called me the other day. She told me about what happened."

Mike's face reddened with embarrassment.

"Son, you can't be acting like that. You scared the kids. You scared Vanessa. She told me that she couldn't have you be like that again, not in front of the kids."

"Fuck, Dad. Really? Fucking really? You are going to drop this fucking huge bomb on me and then attack me? For fuck sake, what do you want from me?" shouts Mike, drawing the attention of other patrons in the restaurant.

"My whole life is fucking falling apart. First, I get kicked out of the Army for being a fucking cripple.I can't do my job. I can't take care of my men. I'm a fucking soldier, and soldiers fight wars. What is a soldier if he can't fight a war?"

"As for me and Vanessa, who knows what's gonna happen between us? I love her, but can I really forgive her betrayal? Can she forgive mine? I have a child with Em. A child I thought I'd lost."

Mike catches a brief shift in Tomas's face at the mention of his child with Em.

The waitress comes to the table and asks Mike to calm down; he is making a scene and scaring the other customers.

"No, I will not calm down. Look, everybody. Look at the fucking sideshow freak." Mike rips off his shirt and turns to show them all his scarred, war-torn body.

A few audible gasps come from the diners in the restaurant.

Tomas gets up and grabs Mike. "Son, put your shirt on, and get outside before they call the cops."

"Fuck them, the cops, and fuck you too. You come here and unload all this shit on me. Fuck you, and fuck this place. I'll be outside." Mike grabs his walking cane and makes his way to the door. As he exits the building, he turns and gives everyone the middle finger; then he walks to the car.

Tomas pays the bill and apologizes profusely to everyone. He asks that they not call the cops and tries to explain the situation.

The restaurant owner agreed, sympathizing with Tomas and understanding the effects war has on a person.

Tomas thanks them and exits the establishment to meet Mike in the car. On the car ride back to Mike's apartment, the tension and silence is thick enough to cut with a knife.

As they neared the Fisher House, thinking he already knew the answer, Mike finally asked the question that had been bothering him, "Did you know Em still had the child?"

Tomas cleared his throat and answered, "Yes."

Mike slowly shook his head and said, "Why didn't you tell me?"

Tomas looked at him and responded, "I am a man of my word."

"It's funny; Em told me that same thing, word for word. And now it makes perfect sense; I know what she meant. When she told me you were a man of your word, I assumed that was about you calling her if anything serious ever happened to me. But now I see that she meant if anything ever happened to her too."

"We're here; you can get out," Mike said as they pulled up to Tomas's car.

"Son, I'm sorry. I didn't mean—"

"Save it, Dad," Mike said as he cut off Tomas.

Tomas shook his head and said, "I love you, son. And to answer your question about who you are if not a soldier, you have to remember that you weren't always a soldier. You are my son. And who you are after being a soldier is a husband, a father, and still my son." Tomas closed Mike's car door and got in his car. He pulled out of the parking lot as Mike watched him drive away.

Mike enters his Fisher House apartment and heads straight for his pills. Then he makes his way to the refrigerator and pulls out an ice-cold beer. In one gulp, he downs the beer. Then grabs another…and another…and another. After drinking four beers in a row, he heads to the couch and plops down.

Mike buries his face in his hands and starts to violently cry, overwhelmed by the weight of everything that happened, everything that was going to happen…just everything. He wanted to call his dad and apologize. Tell him he was sorry and that he didn't mean to say those horrible things. As that feeling slowly passed, in crept a feeling of numbness.

As he sinks into a drunken stupor, Mike's last thoughts are, *Maybe things would just be better if I weren't here. I can't hurt anyone if I'm not here.*

Chapter 27

Mike was just finishing up with his physical-therapy appointment when his phone started to vibrate. Carson's and Mike's faces were on the screen. Mike turned to his physical therapist, Dave, and asked, "Sorry, Dave. Can you give me a second?"

"You know the deal; phones are to be off during therapy, and you know the consequences for breaking the rules," Dave responded while pointing to the sign posted above the gym's door.

Mike nodded his head and excitedly answered the phone, "'Ey, dick. I see you finally made it back."

Carson answered in his North Carolina accent, "Yeah, man. We made it back a few weeks ago. We've all been on block leave and spending time with the fams."

"Shit, man, that's good to hear. How was the rest of the tour?"

"Wasn't like the good ol' days. Had a rough patch, but nothing we couldn't handle. The boys all came back, which is good, you know."

Thinking about all of the excitement and fun firefights he'd missed, Mike's heart raced.

"Anyways, man, I was wondering if you would like to come by the house this weekend. The wife and I are having a barbecue and wanted to see if you and Vanessa could swing by with the kids."

"Yeah, dude, I'll definitely be there, but I'll be riding solo. Vanessa took off north for a few weeks to get everything ready for when I get out."

"No worries, man. We are gonna have a few of the guys over from the platoon also. I know they'd love to see you."

"Aight, man. Thanks for hitting me up. I'll be there this weekend. See you soon, brother."

"See you soon," repeated Carson.

Mike could barely contain his excitement after hanging up the phone.

"Good call?" asked Dave.

"Yeah, I'll get to see my brothers in a few days."

"That's good. Now, time to pay the consequences for breaking the rules."

Mike laughed and said, "A few extra exercises is worth it. Especially if they are going to help get me back into fighting shape again." Mike quickly completed his exercises and then made his way to his apartment.

It had been a week since the episode with Tomas at the restaurant. Mike had isolated himself from everyone, leaving him alone with his thoughts. Spending time with his brothers would be a welcome distraction.

The next few days seemed like an eternity to Mike. Since the day he'd had his meltdown, Mike had been trying to cut back on his drinking and the pain medication.

Finally, Saturday came, and Mike was excited to see his brothers. He left San Antonio late in the afternoon, to arrive at Carson's house just after five o'clock. He was met with huge hugs and an ice-cold beer. Chris, Carson, and Lucas were there, along with a few of the other guys from the platoon. They were all hanging out by the barbecue grill.

"Damn, son, you've gotten small!" said Lucas.

Chris chimed in, "Bro, you look so much better than the last time I saw you. I mean, you still look like shit."

Mike let out a huge laugh and responded, "Well, dick, if it had been Carson or Lucas patching me up, I would have ended up a lot prettier."

They all laughed and quickly changed the subject.

Mike asked, "So catch me up on all that happened after I was evac'd out. Lucas, did you and that chick ever find someone to share with?"

Lucas started blushing and quickly answered, "'Ey, shut up, man. That was an invitation for you alone."

Carson chimed in, "Wait, what? What is Mike talking about?"

"Aw shit, y'all didn't know about Lucas?"

Chris answered, "Nope. What did this fucker forget to tell us."

"Oh shit, let me tell you…" Mike began to recount in vivid detail the time he walked in on Lucas mid-thrust at the aid station.

They took turns, alternating between laughing and taking potshots at Lucas. Lucas laughed along with them and tried to defend himself when possible.

Early in the evening, the topics of conversation were lighthearted and mostly consisted of catching up on how everyone was doing and how each of their families had been. But as the night progressed and alcohol started flowing more freely, conversations took on more serious tones.

The closeness of the guys was equally matched by how tight the wives and girlfriends were. Prior to deployment, the more seasoned guys took turns hosting family cookouts for the entire platoon. The cookouts usually lasted well into the early morning hours. The wives looked out for the members of the platoon by driving people home if needed. Those who stayed the night woke up the next morning and made breakfast for everyone and helped nurse any guys who were hungover.

Mike took a look at his watch and read the time out loud, "Fuck, it's 0130."

"Yeah. Fuck, man, it's good seeing you. I'm glad you came," said Carson.

Mike looks around and notices that Carson and he are the only ones still up. "Look at these lightweights. Fucking pathetic!" Mike shouts.

"It wasn't the same after you left, man. Chris was a fucking wreck. Not knowing if you were gonna make it really fucked with him."

Mike took a sip of the beer he had been nursing for the last hour and said, "Bro, I didn't even know what happened. The last thing I remember was the look on Chris's face and then feeling heat on my right side."

"Damn, man, sounds intense."

"Right, but between me and you, all this shit doesn't feel real. And I don't know what to fucking do."

"What do you mean?"

"I mean, like, I'm here, but I don't feel like I'm here. I mean, my fucking life is falling apart. They are discharging me because I won't heal good enough to do my job. Vanessa and I are trying to make it work, but who knows how long that's gonna last. And then, if shit wasn't fucked up enough, I have a kid with a woman that I've loved since high school."

Carson takes a big gulp of his mixed drink, Seven and Seven, then starts, "So what you gonna do, man? I mean, I know it feels like your world is crashing down around you. But *you* have the power to control *you*. You and I both know the Army will chew you up and spit you out. It doesn't think twice about giving you the big green weenie wrapped in sandpaper and no lube. But you can still do right by you and take care of you."

Mike reflected on what Carson said, and then he thought about his actions toward Em, Vanessa, the kids, and his old man, before answering, "You know what, man…you're right. I need to focus on me. It's like I have this dark void within me. And no matter what I do to fill it, it just keeps growing and growing. I really think I just need to take some time to myself and figure this out. You know, like that song said."

Carson looks at Mike quizzically. "Song?"

"You know…" Mike claps his hand to the beat of "Tainted Love."

Carson smiles…then laughs. "You're an idiot, man."

Mike continues, "I need to get away." Then he takes on a more serious tone with Carson and asks, "'Ey, brother. If I did ever decide to check out, can you promise me, Carson, to help take care of things?"

Carson, in his inebriated state, missed the seriousness in Mike's voice, but he answered, "you know you are my brother, and I will take care of anything you need me to."

"Well, brother, on that note, I really do need to get out of here."

Carson responded, "Oh, we're starting now? I thought you meant later."

Mike laughed and shook his head.

"You're not staying? All these fucks passed out here, so the guest bedroom is free," said Carson.

"Is that the same bed from two years ago?"

"Yeah, why?"

"Yeah, I'm not sleeping there after what Lucas and his flavor of the week did there. Plus, I already have a hotel room just down the road. I would sleep at my house, but there is nothing in there since we are planning to move back north."

"What did Lucas do in my guest room?"

Mike just laughed and answered, "Ask him in the morning when he wakes up."

Mike gets up and walks to his car. Carson follows behind him, extending again the offer to stay the night. Mike declines and gets in his car to go to a fictitious hotel room, when in reality he is driving back to San Antonio.

Mike hid his true feelings from everyone that evening. Even amongst his closest friends, he felt alone and isolated. Staying there with them and waking up the next morning to eat breakfast would have been too painful a reminder of what he would eventually lose forever.

Mike managed to get to within forty-five minutes of the city limits before he pulled over. *Fuck, I'm not gonna make it any farther.* Mike grabbed his cell phone and dialed the only number he could remember.

The phone rings, and a man answers, "Hello, mijo, is everything okay?"

"Dad, I'm fucked up. I'm so fucked up," Mike manages to say.

"Oh, son. Where are you?"

"I'm about forty-five minutes from the house. I can try to make it home," Mike says, sobbing, "but I'm fucked up. God, what the fuck is wrong with me?"

"Listen, son," Tomas says in a calm and soothing voice, "pull over and tell me where you are."

"I'm at the Walmart just outside the city limits."

"Okay, stay there. I'm gonna get off the phone really quickly. I need to call someone to come get you." Tomas hangs up the phone.

About ten minutes pass before Tomas finally calls Mike back. "Son, stay put. Someone is coming for you. They should be there in about an hour. Hold tight."

"Ok, Dad. I'm sorry. I'm so sorry for being a fuckup. I'm sorry for letting you down. I can't do anything right.

I'm a piece-of-shit son. I'm a piece-of-shit father. A piece-of-shit man."

"Hey, hey, son, stop that. You are not a disappointment. And don't worry about what happened the other day. You are my son, and I will always love and forgive you. I will always be here for you, no matter what. As long as I'm alive, I will be here for you."

"Dad, I'm just so tired. I'm so tired. It's like…" Mike started, but drifted off before he could finish his thought.

"Mike…Mike…" Tomas shouted, but he could not get a response from Mike. When Tomas heard Mike snore, his fears subsided slightly.

About forty-five minutes passed as Tomas sat quietly on the phone, listening to a passed-out Mike sleep. Then Tomas heard a knocking on what he guessed was Mike's window. Mike stirred a bit, but did not answer. Tomas then heard a series of honks that woke up Mike.

"Okay, Dad, they are here. I'm safe. I'll talk to you later. 'Kay, love you, bye."

Mike hangs up the phone and is assisted into a small SUV. Mike didn't recognize the vehicle, and in his drunken state, he could not see the person who was helping him into the car. Mike just concentrated on the calming voice. The soothing voice. A voice that sounded very familiar.

Mike pours himself into the front seat of the SUV and buckles up. "Thank you," Mike blurts out before slipping into an unconscious state.

The person looks at Mike and then looks in the back seat of the SUV, at the sleeping boy in his car seat. Em picks up the phone and calls Tomas. "Mr. P., I have Mike. I'm gonna take him to my house and let him sleep. I will bring him back to his car when he wakes up."

"Thank you, Emily. I owe you one. Mike is just a little lost right now. Hopefully, soon he will find his way."

"No worries, Mr. P. You know I love Mike, and I will always be here for him."

Em starts her SUV and makes her way home.

Chapter 28

Mike wakes up dripping in sweat, screaming. Instinctively, he starts looking for his M4 and his body armor. He looks around and doesn't recognize where he is. Not recognizing his surroundings makes Mike panic even more.

Suddenly, he hears a familiar sound—a crying child—and it snaps him back to the present. He starts to slow his breathing and picks an item across the room to focus on. It is the only thing that he can see clearly in the moonlit room. A small heart-shaped frame with a picture of a baby boy in it. He focuses on it and starts to calm down.

In the distance, Mike can hear the crying start to subside. A soft, melodic humming fills the night air. It reminds him of both the first and last times he heard that tune. It is a melody Em hums to fall asleep.

A frightening thought enters Mike's mind, *Did me and Em make love again?* Mike desperately tries to recall the events from earlier in the night. He can only remember up to a few hours after arriving at Carson's house. *Fuck, what did I do?*

A cold chill runs down Mike's back, causing him to shiver. He looks down and sees that he is in his spandex boxer shorts. *What the fuck happened to my clothes? Why am I here?* Mike scrambles to find answers, but is only met with a mental wall of darkness.

Mike focuses on the soft humming that is filling the room. He opens the bedroom door and follows the sound to the door of a nursery room. The door is cracked slightly, allowing Mike to peek inside, where he sees Em bathed in moonlight, which surrounds her in a silvery glow. Her silk robe clings to her body, highlighting the curves.

She is even more beautiful than the day I first saw her.

Em is standing in the center of the room, gently swaying and humming while caressing a child. From what Mike can tell, the child cannot be much older than a year; he is fighting sleep, but rapidly losing the battle. Mike shifts his weight outside the door, trying to get a better look.

The floorboards creek underneath him, catching Em's attention. The child shifts in Em's arms and quickly settles back down.

Em looks toward the door and sees Mike peeking through the crack. With a slight nod of her head, she motions for Mike to come in. As Mike cautiously enters the room so he won't wake the child up again, Em whispers, "Mike, I want you to meet our son, Miguel."

Hearing Em say "our son" sets a wave of emotions crashing within Mike. He walks up behind Em and wraps his arms around her and their son. Mike lowers his head, rests it on Em's shoulders, and begins to match her sway. Em tilts her head back, resting it on Mike's chest, leaning slightly toward his head. Their cheeks softly touch.

It only lasts a few minutes, but for Mike it seems much longer. In those few minutes, he feels something he hasn't felt in a lifetime—peace. Standing in the middle of that room, holding Em and their son, Mike once again believes that all is right in the world and that everything will be okay.

All too soon, Em turns her head slightly, softly kisses Mike's cheek, and whispers, "I have to lay him down."

Mike removes his arms from around Em and backs up, all the way to the door. He watches as Em leans over and places their son in his bed. She then turns, grabs

Mike by the hand, and walks him out of the baby's room and back to the room he woke up in.

Em says, "You can stay in the guest room tonight."

Mike nods in acknowledgment. A myriad of questions his head.

Em can see on Mike's face that he wants to say something. "We can talk in the morning," she whispers.

"Okay," Mike whispers as he turns, enters the guest room, and then slowly starts to close the door behind him.

Em walks toward her room, but stops halfway, and looks back toward Mike. "Mike," she calls out quietly so as not to wake their son.

Mike turns toward Em. "Yes?"

"Good night, my love," she whispers.

Mike's heart flutters, and he smiles. "Good night," he answers back as he closes the door to his room the rest of the way and heads straight for the bed. Confused by Em's actions, he lies in bed, thinking about what just happened.

Was it too much? Did I read this situation wrong? Round and round, his thoughts circle until he starts to fall asleep.

Just before slipping into a deep sleep, Mike hears the door open and feels the covers move. Em crawls into the bed and makes herself comfortable next to Mike. Mike waits for her to settle before leaning down, kissing Em sweetly on the lips, and whispering, "Good night, my love."

Em adjusts her head to rest it on Mike's chest, listening to his heartbeat. Mike wraps his arm around her, holding her close, and they both drift off to sleep.

Chapter 29

Mike is jolted awake by the early birds singing their rhythmic songs. His head is throbbing, and his mouth is dry, lips crusted. Mike's body aches and screams in pain from his injuries. He looks for his pain pills at the side of the bed. *Shit, they are not here.* Nevertheless, he continues to scan the room.

Em shifts in the bed, moaning slightly. This stops Mike's search for his pills. He sits on the side of the bed, staring in awe at his sleeping angel.

Mike hears his son begin to stir and wake. He quietly gets out of bed, careful not to wake Em, and makes his way to Miguel's room. Lifting him out of the bed, he whispers, "Hey there, mijo. You don't know me, but I'm your dad."

Upon hearing Mike's voice, Miguel coos. Almost as if, instinctively, he knows Mike is his father.

"What do you say that we let Mama sleep and just spend some guy time, you and I?" Mike gently bounces Miguel on his hip. Together, they walk downstairs and make their way to the kitchen.

Mike sits Miguel in his high chair and opens up the refrigerator. He pokes his head in, looking for food to make breakfast. "What does Mama have for us to eat?" Mike pops his head out of the fridge and looks at Miguel. "Looks like you get Cheerios and bananas. And it looks like Mama and me will have some eggs, bacon, and avocado toast."

Miguel bounces in his chair and claps as Mike talks to him. Mike opens random cabinets, looking for cooking utensils so he can begin making breakfast. "Hey, Google, play Pandora at volume three," Mike calls out. A slow nineties rock ballad begins to play, bringing a smile to Mike's face. Mike starts cooking and singing along to the music.

In the upstairs room, Em wakes up to the sounds and smells of breakfast in the air. A huge smile crosses her face. She gets up, makes her way downstairs to the kitchen, and sees Mike singing and dancing at her stove. Seeing Mike happy and dancing makes her feel complete.

Mike turns to look at Miguel. "What do you think? Does Mama like her bacon crispy? Or soggy?"

As Mike held up two pieces of bacon, Miguel giggled and said, "Mama," clapping his hands.

With a big smile, Mike repeats, "Yes, Mama. If I remember correctly, Mama likes crispy bacon."

"You're right. I like my bacon crispy," Em answered.

Mike stops and turns to look at Em, who is standing at the entrance of the kitchen in her silk robe.

"And I like my eggs fluffy," Em continued.

Mike smiled his crooked grin. "Oh, good morning, Miss Fancy."

Em shakes her head and walks into the kitchen, toward Miguel, making baby talk. She leans over and kisses him on the cheek. Then Em moves to Mike and runs her hands from the back of his waist, around toward the front, then up his stomach to his chest. She pulls him into her and holds him tightly, taking in the moment. Em kisses Mike's back, then rests her cheek on it.

Mike grabs her arms, holds them, and he, too, soaks in the moment. "Did you sleep well? I wanted to let you sleep in since I kept you up last night. But this guy had other plans."

Miguel giggles and says, "Mama."

Em reluctantly lets go of Mike and goes to a cabinet to get some plates and glasses so they can eat breakfast. She takes them out and places them on the island countertop. Then sits at the corner of the island and watches Mike.

Mike continues to sing and dance while finishing up breakfast. When the bacon is done, he plates it and puts it on the island. Mike picks up a piece of bacon and feeds it to Em.

She laughs as she bites into it. "Mmm, that's good."

Turning back to the stove, Mike pours the eggs into the hot bacon grease and cooks them. A loud pop comes from the toaster just before the eggs are done. "Ah, perfect timing," says Mike.

"Babe, do you mind getting the juice?" asks Mike.

Realizing what Mike called her, Em gets up and pauses for a brief second before walking to the refrigerator. Before plating the eggs and placing them on the island, Mike also pauses after realizing what he said.

Em pours two glasses of orange juice and sits back down. Mike stands at the corner of the island, next to Em, and serves her the bacon and eggs before serving himself. They stay there, looking at each other, lost in each other's eyes while eating breakfast.

"Ah, um, is there enough for me too?" said Mirasol, Em's mother, as she walked into the kitchen.

Mike blushed and answered, "Of course, Mrs. Sanchez. There is plenty for all of us."

"Good, because it's not every day that Milly has a half-naked man cooking her breakfast," said Mirasol while staring judgmentally at Em.

"Mom," said Em, "stop it. Don't be like that."

"What, mija? It's true; it's not every day you have a strange man in your house, cooking you breakfast," responds Mirasol. She walks to Miguel and gives him a hug and kiss. "How is my little *cielito*?" Then she moves to give Em a hug and kiss. After that, Mirasol stands in front of Mike, looks him up and down for a second before rolling her eyes and leaning in.

Mike leans in as well and cheek kisses both sides of Mirasol's face. "Good morning, Mrs. Sanchez. I hope we didn't wake you while we were cooking breakfast."

"No, I was awake since early this morning when I heard a man screaming in the middle of the night," said Mirasol.

Mike's face reddened in embarrassment.

"*MOM!* Stop it," said Em.

"What? He asked me if he woke me up while he was cooking. I was just answering him," said Mirasol in a condescending tone.

"I'm sorry, ma'am. I-I...uh...I-I..." stuttered Mike, desperately trying to come up with any answer other than the truth.

"Mom, leave him alone. You have to accept it. He is Miguel's father, whether you like it or not," said Em.

"Well, we'll see how much of a father he really is," responded Mirasol.

"Mom, stop it, please," pleaded Em.

"What? What is it you two are doing here? Playing house? Mija, he is married...and not to you. To... another...woman!" Mirasol turns to look at Mike. "And you, what are you thinking? She is not your wife! She is not your girlfriend! You are married. You can't keep waltzing in and out of her life whenever you feel like it—" Mirasol's rant is interrupted by a coughing fit.

Em rushes over to Mirasol. "Mom, let's get you back into bed."

Mike goes to assist Em in taking Mirasol back to her room. He scoops Mirasol into his arms, carries her to her bedroom, and places her on the bed. Em grabs the oxygen tubing and hands it to Mirasol. Mike pulls the covers over Mirasol and tucks her in.

Miguel starts crying, and Em rushes out of the room, heading back to the kitchen to tend to him.

As Mike turns to leave, Mirasol grabs his hand and pulls him back. "Mike, you need to stop breaking my daughter's heart. If you really love her, you need to let her go. You need to promise me that you will let her go. I can't leave this Earth knowing that you still have a hold on her. Promise me."

Mike grabs Mirasol's hand tighter. "Mrs. Sanchez, I've loved your daughter since the day I first laid eyes on her. She was and will always be my first true love. And I have done something I am not proud of for your daughter, so that she could be safe and live the life she deserves." He sighs deeply. "But if this is your dying request, then I will honor and respect it."

"It is. Be a father to your son, like he deserves. But leave Emily alone," responded Mirasol.

Mike bends down, kisses Mirasol's hand, and walks back toward the kitchen.

"Is everything okay? I'm sorry about what my mom said. She's just trying to—" started Em.

Mike interrupts, "No, it's fine. But it's getting late, and I don't want to take up all of your time."

"No, it's okay. I don't have anything planned," said Em.

"Yeah, but I do. I need to get back and run some errands and, uh…you know, take care of some other things," Mike replied.

"Oh, okay…yeah…well, let me get your clothes and grab my keys." Em gets up and heads to the laundry room. "The bathroom's over there," she says, pointing down the hall.

Mike heads to the bathroom, shuts the door, and catches a glimpse of himself in the mirror. *What are you doing?* he thinks to himself, balling his fists until his knuckles turn white. He lets out a soft cry while getting dressed. *Is this what life could be like with Em?*

Mike ponders briefly what could be; then he remembers what he promised Mirasol. *No, it can't be.*

Mike exits the bathroom and heads toward the front door, where Em and Miguel are waiting for him.

"You ready?" asked Em.

"Yeah."

"Well then, let's go," said Em as she opened the door. As Mike walks out and heads toward Em's SUV, Em locks up and grabs Miguel. She secures him in his car seat and then gets in.

Mike sits quietly on the passenger side of the SUV, staring out the window as Em backs out and takes off toward Mike's car.

Chapter 30

Em and Mike ride most of the way in silence. "Um...
Mike...I'm sorry about my mom. She's just..."

"Em, you don't have to apologize. I get it. She's right.
I mean, what the fuck were we doing? What *are* we
doing? We aren't a family. We aren't gonna be one. I'm
not good for you. All I've done since we met is break
your heart. You don't need that in your life."

Em turns to look at Mike. "What? What are you
talking about?"

"Em, let's face it. When we were kids, all I did was
create problems for you. I'm a fucking black hole. I'm

pretty to look at from afar, but anything that comes into my orbit, I destroy."

"What are you talking about? Where is this coming from? You can't tell me that this morning didn't feel right to you. You can't lie to me and tell me that this morning meant nothing to you."

"It wasn't real."

"What?"

Mike could see the heartbreak on Em's face. "Look, I will be here for Miguel. He is my son, and I will be here so he can get to know his dad. But that's it. That's all it can be."

Em stifles her tears and muffles her cry. She will not let Mike see her like this.

Mike started recognizing his surroundings and knew his car was close. He knew that this was his opportunity to do the hardest thing he had ever had to do. "Em, let's just face it. I keep coming back to you because you're my safety net. You are comfortable, and I know you. The more I think about it, that is why I keep coming back to you. It's not fair to you. It's not fair to me. After today, I think it's best that we only speak when it deals with our son."

Mike's words devastated Em. She gripped the steering wheel tightly. "We're here," she said.

Mike opens the door and starts to get out.

"And don't worry about Miguel. He will be fine. Like I told Vanessa, I don't want anything from you. I just wanted you to meet your son. You did that. That's all I wanted."

Mike stops and turns to look at Em. "Is that the way you really want it?"

"Yes, it is."

Mike nods his head slowly. "So be it then." He shuts the door and walks to his car. Then sits in his car and watches Em drive away.

Once she is out of sight, Mike lets loose his emotions and starts punching the steering wheel. "Argh!" he screams at the top of his lungs. "Fuck! Fuck!" After a few minutes of his angry outburst, Mike starts his car, puts it in Drive, and heads to his apartment.

Mike felt as if his whole world shattered after Em pulled away. On the drive home, all Mike could think about was how much of an asshole he was to Em. He replayed what he said to her over and over again. Then he thought about what Mirasol said to him and the promise he'd made to her.

Mike pulls into the parking lot of the Fisher House and sees Vanessa standing by her car, arms crossed and a scowl on her face. *Fuck!* Mike thinks to himself as he parks next to Vanessa's car.

"Hey, babe," Mike says as he exits his car.

"Where the fuck have you been? And why weren't you answering your phone?" screamed Vanessa.

"Babe, calm down. I told you I was going to Carson's house yesterday. I had some beers and crashed at his house. You can call and ask him."

Vanessa stares at Mike. "I'm not gonna call him. That fucker will lie for you. I'm gonna call Jess. She'll tell me the truth."

"Go head; call her. She's gonna tell you what I just told you." He motions for Vanessa to make the call.

Vanessa sits and stares at Mike for a brief moment, then asks, "So then, why didn't you answer your phone? I've been trying to call and text you to let you know I was coming down."

"My phone died last night, and I couldn't charge it because I didn't have a charging cord. It wasn't until I started driving this morning that I was able to charge it with my car charger. I don't want to text or call while driving. I was going to call you when I got back, but you were already here."

Mike walks toward Vanessa, grabs her arms, and pulls her close. "C'mon, babe. I told you that I love you and that I want to be with you. I want us to be a family." Mike leans in to kiss Vanessa on the lips.

She hesitates for a moment before meeting him halfway and returning his kiss.

Mike grabs Vanessa by the hand and leads her to his apartment.

She follows behind him. "Babe, I'm sorry I was acting like that. I was scared. I didn't know where you were. I didn't know if something had happened to you."

Mike stops and turns to Vanessa. " I understand that, babe. And I'm sorry. I should have called before my phone died. I'm trying to do better. I'm trying to *be* better. I'm trying to cut back on drinking and taking pills. I want to be the man I was before for you and the kids."

They get to the door, and Mike opens it. As they walk in, Vanessa looks around the apartment and notices that it is not littered with empty beer cans and liquor bottles.

"How was the drive down?" asked Mike as he walked back to the room to change into a shirt and basketball shorts.

"It was okay. I didn't have the kids with me, so I didn't have to stop very often. Other than just worrying about you, it was good."

Mike walks back into the living room and sits next to Vanessa on the couch. "I'm glad you came down here. I missed you and the kids."

Vanessa smiles and moves close to Mike. "I missed you too. I wanted to surprise you with a visit because, since you've been back, we haven't gotten to spend any quality time together."

Mike smiles. "I know, babe. What do you say we rest up and go to dinner tonight on the Riverwalk?"

"That sounds good. I am tired from the drive. I left at four this morning. I could use a nap," said Vanessa as she got up and walked toward the bedroom.

Mike got up and followed, watching Vanessa strip down to her bra and panties.

Vanessa turns and asks, "Can I borrow a shirt to sleep in?"

Mike goes to the dresser drawer, pulls out a worn-out, grey Army PT shirt, and gives it to Vanessa.

She slips it on and crawls into Mike's bed as he lifts the covers and slides in next to her. She curls up next to him and rests her head on his chest. Vanessa takes her hand and lightly runs it up and down his chest. She turns her head slightly and kisses his skin, sending chills down Mike's body.

Mike shifts, turning toward Vanessa, and kisses the top of her head. "I'm tired, babe, and my body is hurting. I haven't taken my pain pills today."

Vanessa stops and puts her back to Mike.

He grabs her and pulls her into him. "I missed holding you. I missed this."

"Me too."

Mike holds Vanessa tightly as she falls asleep. His thoughts drift to earlier that morning when he was holding Em. Kissing Em. Cuddling Em. He could feel his heart breaking at the thought that he would never know that feeling again.

He looks at Vanessa, sleeping peacefully, and thinks, *I'm such a horrible person for treating Vanessa like this,* as he falls asleep.

Chapter 31

Mike wakes up from his nap and sees Vanessa still lying in bed. He gets up and walks to the kitchen. *Fuck, my body is fucking killing me,* Mike thinks to himself, feeling every inch of his scars shooting him full of electrifying pain. Mike braces his right hand against the wall to help stay his balance and take some weight off his aching joints.

Mike hears a rhythmic vibration sound, like the ringing of a phone. He scans the apartment, trying to locate the source. Following the sound, Mike finally locates it— Vanessa's phone in her purse. Mike picks up the phone to see who is calling. *Unknown number? Who the fuck is calling her? It could be just a wrong number or a telemarketer.*

Mike puts the phone back into Vanessa's purse and goes to the kitchen to take his pain medication. He hears Vanessa begin to wake up in the bedroom and walks toward the side of the bed on which Vanessa is lying. Mike kneels and gets face-to-face with her.

Vanessa slowly opens her eyes and is met with Mike gazing at her. "What time is it?" she asks.

"It's five o'clock."

"How long have you been up?"

"Just a few minutes. My body was hurting, and it woke me up. What time do you want to go get dinner?"

"Soon. I'm a hungry bird."

Mike chuckles and says, "Okay. Well, let's get ready, and we'll head out soon." He leans in, kisses Vanessa, and helps her get up.

Vanessa starts to rise, but then lies back and pulls Mike to her. Mike falls back into bed, rolls over Vanessa, and stops on the other side of the bed. Vanessa rolls with Mike and stops on top of him. She straddles him, pins his arms down to the bed, and starts to grind her hips over Mike's.

"We have some time before we have to get ready," Vanessa says and bites her lower lip. She feels Mike start to get hard as she continues rubbing against him. She leans in to kiss and nibble his neck.

Excited, Mike squirms and moves back and forth as Vanessa continues kissing his body, moving from his neck, down to his chest, and then to his left nipple. She licks and nibbles it, sending shock waves of pleasure surging through him. He lets out a soft moan.

Vanessa continues kissing Mike's body. She makes her way to the opposite nipple and runs her hands along the sides of his body, over the scars from his injuries. She stops, looks at them, and gasps.

Mike noticed Vanessa's shock and stopped her from continuing. Her reaction made him self-conscious about his body and his injuries. He himself had had a difficult time accepting his injuries and the change in his physique. Vanessa's reaction served as a reminder to Mike of how hideous his body was.

At least my outside matches the inside—a horrible monster, Mike thinks to himself. He overpowers Vanessa, grabs her arms, and stops her from continuing to kiss him.

"What's the matter?" asked Vanessa.

"We should get ready. I haven't showered since yesterday, and I'm starting to get really hungry," answers Mike, pushing Vanessa off him, toward the empty side of the bed. Mike gets up, walks around the room, and gathers his clothes so he can shower and get ready for dinner.

Vanessa lies in bed, watching him. *What did I do wrong? Is it 'cause I touched his scars?*

She had seen his body after his injuries, but touching them in person was a new experience. Vanessa felt rejected and shamed by Mike's reaction. Despite being married for years, being intimate with Mike after his ordeal was uncharted territory.

"You coming?" asks Mike before making his way to the bathroom.

Vanessa gets up and follows Mike into the bathroom. She watches as Mike strips down and enters the shower, her eyes fixated on the scars left by the shrapnel and the surgeries he endured during his recovery. She enters the shower after Mike, still fixated on his war-torn body, grabs Mike from behind, pulling him into her naked body, and holds him. The running water masks her tears. She kisses his back and sways gently with Mike in her arms.

Mike holds Vanessa's arms and sways with her. The warm water helps to soothe Mike's aching body. Vanessa's warm embrace helps to calm his mind. Standing there in Vanessa's arms helps to numb the pain from this morning. Helps to make the night shared with Em a distant memory.

Mike pulls away from Vanessa's arms and starts to wash his hair. As he reaches for his loofah, Vanessa swoops in and grabs it. She begins to wash his back for him. Mike turns and does the same for Vanessa.

Then he turns Vanessa around and stands face-to-face with her. He looks deeply into her eyes and says, "Vanessa, I know I am a troubled man. I know I have my faults. But I want you to know"—Mike takes her hand and puts it on his chest, over his heart—"that I love you with all my heart and soul. You make me want to be a better man, father, husband. You deserve the best, and I know the last few years I have not given that to you. I promise you, from this day forward, I will."

Vanessa tears up, "Mi amor, I know I have betrayed your trust. And I have my faults, but if you still want to be with me, and you can forgive me, I promise you that I will be the best version of me for you."

Mike pulls Vanessa in close and hugs her tightly.

"Ah, the water's turning cold. Let's get out." The shower water had gone from warm to freezing cold. They both laugh as they rush to get out from under it.

Mike and Vanessa dry off and finish getting dressed. Mike calls for an Uber to pick them up and take them to eat at the Riverwalk in Downtown San Antonio. On the car ride, they act as they did when they first started dating. Mike can feel the fire being rekindled between Vanessa and him.

"What do you feel like eating?" asked Mike.

Vanessa shrugged her shoulders. "I don't care, as long as I'm with you."

They walk side by side and hand in hand along the river, amongst the crowd of tourists, locals, and military recruits on weekend passes. After a few blocks, they stop at a Mexican restaurant and are seated at a table outside, overlooking the sidewalk.

Vanessa takes a seat with her back to the restaurant and gets comfortable, but Mike remains standing and looking at Vanessa.

"What's the matter? Are you going to sit down?" asked Vanessa.

"Um, can I have that seat, please?"

"Why? You can sit there," said Vanessa as she pointed across the table from her.

Mike could feel his anxiety soar through the roof. "Please. Can I sit there?"

Vanessa could sense Mike's uneasiness, so she got up to avoid a potential outburst. Mike sat in the seat

Vanessa vacated, as Vanessa settled into the seat next to him as the waitress came and took their drink orders.

Dinner was filled with laughter and flirtation, as if they were young lovers. Vanessa told Mike about how the kids were growing and how they were doing in school. She could see in Mike the man with whom she'd fallen in love all those years ago.

"Amor, look at that group of guys over there," said Mike, pointing to four young men walking together in a group.

Vanessa turned to see what Mike was talking about.

"Watch. One of them is going to change steps in three… two…one…"

As Mike's countdown ended, one of the men did a shuffle to get in step with the rest of his group.

Mike let out a little laugh. "Could have been me many years ago."

"No, because you're a rule breaker. Since I've known you, you've always walked your own path."

Mike and Vanessa sat and continued to talk and reconnect well into the night. At nine thirty, Vanessa said, "Amor, let's do something we haven't done in a long time."

"What's that, my love?"

"Let's go dancing. We haven't been dancing since before I was pregnant with Lexi. What do you say?"

"I would love to. I haven't spun you around on a dance floor in years."

They paid for dinner and walked along the river, looking for someplace with a dance floor that wasn't too crowded. After trying a few different bars and clubs, they finally found one. They headed to the bar and ordered a round of shots.

A rhythm-and-blues song started playing as they entered the club. "Oh my God, I love this song," Vanessa shouts in Mike's ear as she grabs his hand and starts dragging him to the dance floor.

Mike and Vanessa spend the next few hours dancing the night away. They occasionally break away from the dance floor to down more shots.

After a while, Mike could feel his body begin to throb. He needed to take a break. "I have to take a piss," he shouted in Vanessa's ear. "I'll be right back."

Mike then walked off the dance floor, limped to the restroom, and waited in line to take a piss. He finally made it to a urinal and posted his hand on the wall in front of him, taking some weight off his body. He finished urinating, washed his hands, and walked back out to the dance floor.

The club's loud music and flashing lights started making Mike's head throb. He could feel his pulse accelerating and his chest tightening. Sweat started pouring from his forehead. The crowded club's walls began to close in on him.

Vanessa noticed Mike had not returned from the restroom and started to get worried. She walked around the club, looking for him. She found him standing outside of the club, resting on the rail of the sidewalk.

"Hey, you okay?" asked a concerned Vanessa.

Mike nodded his head and said, "Yeah, I...uh... I just had to get some air."

"I'm sorry. I should have known that the club might be too much."

"No, it's okay. I wanted to do it. I wanted to do something you love."

"I just want to spend time with you. *That* is what I love."

Mike smiled his crooked grin.

Vanessa said, "Let's order an Uber and head back to the apartment."

Mike nodded and pulled out his phone.

The car ride home was fairly quiet. Vanessa slid next to Mike, placed her hand on the inside of his thigh, and ran it up to his groin. Mike turned and looked at her. She laid her head on his shoulder and rubbed his member, feeling it engorge.

They arrived at the Fisher House and walked to Mike's apartment. Vanessa, leading the way, reached back for a handful of Mike's manhood. They stopped outside Mike's door, and he fumbled for his keys, finally fishing them out of his pocket and unlocking the door.

Vanessa rushes through the door, pulling Mike in behind her. She pushes Mike against the door, slamming it shut. Vanessa drops to her knees and undoes Mike's pants, taking out his member. She thrusts it into her mouth and starts sucking rhythmically.

Mike moans, feeling Vanessa's soft, moist mouth surrounding his manhood. "Oh God. That feels so good, baby," said Mike. Vanessa continues her rhythmic motion for a few minutes before Mike pulls her off his member and stands her up. He twirls her around, pushes her against the door, and rips off her shirt; then he undoes the button on her jeans. Vanessa helps Mike pull down her skintight jeans and panties.

Mike follows the curves of Vanessa's long, toned legs, and then he drops to his knees and begins to kiss her under her belly button. Mike looks up and sees Vanessa staring down at him. Locking eyes, he kisses and nibbles from her belly button down to her pubic region.

Vanessa gasps as Mike kisses the inner creases of her hips. "Don't stop, babe," she moans. When Vanessa can no longer stand Mike's teasing, she grabs his head and directs it to her womanhood. Mike instantly licks and nibbles Vanessa's spot, sending her into waves of ecstasy.

In a swift and graceful move, Mike stands, throws Vanessa over his shoulder, and makes his way to the bedroom. Arriving at the foot of the bed, Mike flings Vanessa down on it. She lands faceup, looking at Mike, her feet toward him. Vanessa lets out a giggle. Mike crawls from the foot of the bed, up, until he is in between Vanessa's waiting legs.

He slides his manhood into her, taking her breath away, and slowly begins to thrust. Vanessa's body quivers with pleasure as Mike continues to thrust deeper and harder. Faster and faster, Mike moves his hips.

Vanessa digs her nails into his back and bites Mike's shoulder. "Don't stop, baby. Oh my God, don't stop," said Vanessa, but she noticed the motion start to slow as Mike's manhood softened.

Mike kept thrusting and thrusting, but could feel himself losing his hard erection. He started to cry, but he kept thrusting until his once hard member was flaccid. Still crying, Mike peeled himself off Vanessa. Mad, he struck the side of the bed, next to Vanessa, over and over.

Vanessa sat up, wrapped her arms around Mike, and lay back down, bringing his back to her chest, spooning Mike. "Sshhh…sshhh…it's okay, baby. It's okay. You've been through a lot, and this happens. It will take time to get to how we were."

Mike rolls over onto his side and faces Vanessa. "Fuck, why do you want to be with me if I can't even be a man. I can't fuck like a man."

"Baby, I love you. And my love for you is more than a physical thing." She held him as he cried and dealt with the trouble he had performing. "Shh, my love. Shh, it's okay," Vanessa repeats while rubbing Mike's neck and shoulders until he falls asleep.

* * *

Later that night…

Mike wakes up in a cold sweat, his heart racing and his body aching. He looks at the bedside clock—three thirty. Mike turns his head to the window and sees that it is still pitch-black. He shakes his head as the taste of blood fills his mouth.

Fuck. He rubs his shoulders and knees and slowly stands up and makes his way to the bedroom door. He looks back at Vanessa. Mike smiles at seeing her beautiful body lying there as she sleeps peacefully.

Mike hobbles down the hallway to the kitchen to get his pain medication. A buzzing vibration screams out in the dead of the night, catching Mike's attention. *Where the fuck is that coming from?* Mike asks himself.

He walks to Vanessa's purse, and the buzzing grows louder. Mike reaches into the purse and looks at Vanessa's phone. The call appears to be from the same caller as before. Mike looks at the phone's screen and contemplates accepting the call. He brings the phone towards his head, but stops midway. "Nah, I have to trust her," Mike mumbles to himself and puts the phone down.

Mike turns to head back to the bedroom. He takes two steps before the phone starts buzzing again. Mike turns and walks back to the purse. He picks up the phone and accepts the call, but does not say anything.

A man's voice comes from the other side of the phone. "Vanessa…please don't hang up. Vanessa, are you there? I can hear you breathing," says the voice.

Mike clears his throat and hangs up the phone. He softly cries as he makes his way back to the bedroom. His heart is shattered into a million pieces. Mike crawls back in bed and lies there, staring at the ceiling.

Vanessa feels Mike getting back in bed and moves closer to him. She places her arm around him and falls back asleep.

Staring at the ceiling, Mike contemplated what he was going to do. His thoughts ran rampant. *She lied to me. She's playing me for a fool.* The more Mike thought about it, the madder he got.

Mike stayed awake for a few more hours, playing out different scenarios in his head, until he passed out from the effects of his medications.

Chapter 32

Morning comes, and Mike is up at first light. His shocking discovery did not let him rest as much as he would have liked. He moves around the room to gather his workout clothes.

After the phone call last night, Mike had a lot to think about. *What the fuck am I gonna do? A run should help clear my mind. I gotta take it easy though. It's been a long time since I've tried to run. I can't go running six-minute miles like I used to,* he thought.

Mike puts on his running clothes, grabs his headphones, and is out the door. He takes off at a pace slightly quicker than a brisk walk. He holds that pace for about a quarter of a mile before his body starts to ache. The cool fall air stings his lungs.

Mike pushes himself a little faster at about the half-mile mark. He keeps the pace up for a few minutes, until he feels his chest tighten and his legs scream in pain. Mike slows down to a walk and starts coughing violently. He finally comes to a stop and begins to vomit. Mike can't tell if he is vomiting because of his exertion while running, or the sickening feeling from answering Vanessa's phone. Tears roll down his cheek and sting his eyes.

Mike turns and walks back to the apartment with his head hung low in defeat. *Fuck, I can't even run a mile. How the fuck am I expected to provide for my family? Now, I can't blame Vanessa for cheating on me again.*

Mike finally makes it back to the apartment and finds Vanessa in his shirt, making breakfast.

Vanessa walks from the stove to the door to greet Mike with a good-morning kiss.

Mike pulls away slightly, saying, "Sorry, babe, I'm all sweaty."

Vanessa is taken aback by Mike's actions. "Couldn't sleep?"

"Nah, I couldn't get comfortable. My body kept hurting."

"I'm sorry, love. I wouldn't have asked to go dancing if I'd known that you'd be hurting this bad."

"It's fine. I need to try to start doing things like I used to. What do you want to do today?"

Vanessa shrugged her shoulders. "I don't know. We don't have to do anything if your body is hurting."

After the previous night's phone call, Mike could not stand the thought of being confined to the apartment with Vanessa. The thought burned him at his core. *Just let it go. I'm sure there is an explanation,* he thought to himself.

"How about we go downtown and have some lunch and maybe catch a movie? I really don't feel like being cooped up in the house," suggested Mike.

"I like that, babe. I love spending time with you."

Vanessa finished making breakfast, and they ate at the small, round kitchen table. Mike was doing his best to act as if nothing were bothering him, but Vanessa could sense something was wrong. She dared not ask him because she was scared of how Mike would react. So breakfast was eaten with minimal conversation.

After breakfast was done, Vanessa got up from the table. "You done with this, baby?" asked Vanessa, pointing to Mike's dishes.

"Yeah."

Vanessa picks up the dishes and walks to the sink to clean up.

"I'm gonna hop in the shower real quick," said Mike as he gets up and takes off his shirt. Before making his way to the bedroom, he stops at the kitchen counter and grabs his pain medication. He opens up each bottle and pours one to two pills from each into his hand. In one fell swoop, he throws them to the back of his throat and swallows them with a big gulp. Then, without a word, Mike makes his way to the bathroom to take a shower.

After showering, Mike dries off the bathroom mirror with his towel. He pauses for a moment, staring at his reflection. Mike turns so he can see his right side. He examines his body and closely analyzes the patterns of his scars. *Goddamn, that's hideous. I've lost so much muscle mass. I'm so fucking small.*

Mike turns to the left, continuing to examine his body. After a few minutes, he turns again and stands directly in front of the mirror. *Who am I? Who is this staring back at me?*

Mike still can't believe how much he has changed. He thinks back to a few weeks before he was injured, to when Lucas and he were working out at the gym on the FOB. They took off their shirts and had a flex-off in the middle of the gym. *That man looks nothing like this one,* thought Mike.

A knock on the bathroom door brings Mike back to the present.

"Babe, can you open up. I have to pee," said Vanessa from the other side of the door.

"Yeah, give me a second." Mike unlocks the door.

Vanessa rushes in. She sits on the toilet and starts to pee. "Babe, what time do you want to go to the movies? What do you want to see?"

Mike, annoyed with the barrage of questions, snaps, "Fuck! I don't know. Let's just fucking see when we get there."

Vanessa is shocked by Mike's response. "Okay, I'm sorry. I just wanted to know."

Mike closes his eyes and takes a deep breath. "No, I'm sorry. I'm just not feeling like myself today. Let's see when we get there, okay?"

"Okay," answers Vanessa as she finishes using the toilet.

Mike walks out of the bathroom and puts on a pair of old basketball shorts and an old grey Army physical-training shirt; then he heads to the living room. He sits down and flips on the TV, looking for something to watch.

Vanessa follows him and sits down next to him. She lifts her feet up and places them on the unoccupied couch cushion next to her; then she lays her head in Mike's lap.

Mike looks down at Vanessa and rubs his hand along her side. *I wonder how many times she did this with that fucking dude,* he thinks.

They sat together on the couch for a few hours in silence. All the while, Mike was lost in his own thoughts. He kept festering about the calls from earlier that morning and the day before.

"Babe, are you starting to get hungry?" asked Vanessa.

"Yeah, a bit."

"Well, let's get ready to go," suggested Vanessa.

They get up and get dressed. Before leaving the apartment, Mike walks to the kitchen counter and takes another round of pills. He grabs his keys, and together Vanessa and Mike make their way to Mike's car.

"Babe, do you really think you should be driving? You just took your medication?" asked Vanessa.

Mike glares at Vanessa. "I'm fine to drive. I just took it in case we do a lot of walking. So I won't hurt so much when I get back."

"Mike, I'm just—"

"Do you want to go or not?" interrupted Mike.

Vanessa was again taken aback at Mike's response. But she got in the car anyway, and they proceeded toward Downtown San Antonio. After parking near the River-center Mall, they made their way to the mall.

"Oh, I feel like eating at the Brazilian steakhouse," stated Vanessa.

"You sure? I don't think it's very good."

"No, it is, and it will be nice."

"Fine," scoffed Mike.

So they make their way toward the restaurant. Vanessa reaches for Mike's hand, but he pulls it away and puts it in his pocket. Vanessa turns to look at Mike. He ignores her and keeps walking.

Arriving at the restaurant, they are greeted by the host. "Table for two?" the host asked.

"Yeah, that's how many you see, right?" snapped Mike.

Vanessa's face reddened with embarrassment.

"My apologies, sir. Please, this way," responded the host.

"Can we have a table toward the back?" asked Mike.

"Of course, sir."

The host seats Mike and Vanessa in the back of the restaurant. Mike takes the front-facing chair, putting his back to the wall so he can watch the door. Vanessa seats herself next to him.

Vanessa waits until the host is out of earshot before saying, "Mike, why are you being an asshole?"

"What? He was asking stupid questions. He only saw the two of us."

"We could have been part of a party."

"Whatever."

A waitress dressed in black slacks and a white shirt with a black vest approached their table. "Welcome, have you been here before?" asked the waitress.

"Yeah," said Mike.

"Yes," answered Vanessa.

"Oh good. What can I get y'all to drink?" said the waitress.

"I'll have a glass of the house red," said Vanessa.

"I'll have a caipirinha," said Mike.

Vanessa looks at Mike with a concerned expression.

Mike mouths, *"What?"*

Vanessa shakes her head.

"Okay, so that's a house red and a caipirinha. I'll bring that right out. You know how this works. The green side of the card means the gauchos will bring meats to the table. Red means they will leave you alone to eat." The waitress turns to walk away and place their drink orders.

"Mike, do you really think that you should be drinking with your medication?" asked Vanessa.

"It's fine. Fuck. We are gonna eat and watch a movie. I'll be fine by the time we head home."

Vanessa sensed Mike was starting to get agitated, so she let it go.

Mike and Vanessa ate and made small talk during lunch. Every time the waitress came to the table, Mike ordered another drink.

After the fourth drink, Vanessa was compelled to say something. "Mike, don't you think you've had enough?"

"I'm fine, for fuck sake."

"I'm just saying you know you're not supposed to be mixing your medication with alcohol. And you know that you're not supposed to be driving while on that medication."

"Why don't you just let me fucking be. God, I'm not your child. You don't need to mother me."

"I'm just concerned. And I'm worried for your safety. You've been taking a lot of risks. And I just don't want anything to happen to you."

Mike looked at Vanessa. "Oh, *now* you care about me. *Now* you care about how I am doing."

"What? What do you mean?"

"Nothing. Never mind. I don't feel like watching a movie anymore. I just want to go home."

"Fine!"

Mike flags down the waitress and asks for the check. He pays, gets up, and quickly walks toward the door, leaving Vanessa at the table.

Vanessa hurries to catch up to Mike. "Mike, wait… please," calls out Vanessa, but Mike keeps walking at his fast pace. "Mike, slow down!" Vanessa calls out again, jogging to catch up with Mike.

Mike, in his pissed-off state, tuned out everything around him. All Mike could focus on was the phone call on Vanessa's phone. All he heard was the man's voice on the other end of the line.

Vanessa finally catches up to Mike and grabs his arm. That scares Mike since he is lost in his head, inebriated, and unaware of his surroundings. Mike whips around with a clenched fist ready to strike the person who grabbed his arm. His fist gets within inches of Vanessa's face. Mike stops at the last second before striking Vanessa.

Vanessa screams and drops to the ground, cowering.

Her screams grab the attention of a passerby. "Hey, big man! You think you're tough, hitting a woman?" shouted the Good Samaritan.

Mike turns his focus from Vanessa on the ground to the Good Samaritan. "Mind your fucking business."

Vanessa scrambles to get to her feet and gets in between Mike and the Good Samaritan. "Mike! No, Mike. Let's go to the car," pleaded Vanessa.

"No, honey, this man needs to be taught a lesson on how to treat a lady," shouted the Good Samaritan.

Mike stopped shouting and stood very still. He glared at the approaching man. Mike slid his hand to his right hip pocket and pulled out his pocketknife. Without making a sound, Mike opened the knife and calmly said, "I am going to ask you one more time. Mind your fucking business, and walk away."

The man stopped approaching Mike. Something in the way Mike suddenly became eerily calm sent chills down his spine. "Ma'am, you don't need to be with a man that will treat you like that," said the Good Samaritan.

"It's my fault. I shouldn't have snuck up on him. He just got back from a deployment. He is still adjusting to being back," cried Vanessa.

The man looked at Mike and then Vanessa. After hesitating, he walked away.

"C'mon, Mike, let's go before someone calls the cops," Vanessa said as she grabbed Mike's arm and rushed him to the parking garage where they'd parked.

They got in their car and left. The car ride home was uncomfortable and silent. Mike concentrated on driving, and Vanessa cried quietly while staring out the window.

"I gotta make a stop before we go home," Mike finally said. He pulled into a gas station and disappeared inside.

A few minutes passed; then Mike exited with two cases of beer. He opens the driver's-side passenger door and puts the beer inside. He forcefully closes the door, gets back in the driver's seat, and starts driving again.

Mike pulls into the parking lot of the Fisher House. He gets out, grabs the beer, and walks to his apartment, Vanessa cautiously following. Mike opens the door and shuts it behind him, right in Vanessa's face.

Vanessa opens the door. "What the fuck was that, Mike? Why are you acting this way?"

"Why the fuck do you care? What fucking game are you playing?"

"I thought we were gonna have a nice day. Eat some lunch and watch a movie. Last night went so good. I thought we were doing good."

"Are we? Are we doing good? Is that what you think?"

"Mike, what changed?"

"I changed. I am not the same man I once was. I don't look the same. My body's not the same. I can't even fuck the same way I used to. Why the fuck do you want to be with me?" Mike shouts. "I am me and I don't even want to be me." Mike let out a primal scream and banged his fists on his chest, then ripped off his shirt. "Look at this. Look at these. I am a fucking mess. I can't walk, run, or even just get through the fucking day without shoveling pills down my throat."

"'Cause I love you, babe. 'Cause you are the father of our children. I don't care that you don't look like you did. I didn't fall in love with you for your body. I love you for you."

"Don't give me that shit. You don't fucking love me. You are just using me until you find something better. I'm not fucking stupid. I know you're still seeing that fucking dude," shouted Mike.

"What? No, I'm not," defended Vanessa.

Mike got in Vanessa's face. "Don't you fucking lie to me. I know you are still talking to him. Don't play me for a fucking fool. He called you twice yesterday from a unknown number. Once, while you were taking a nap, and then again at three in the morning," shouted Mike.

"What? Mike let me explain—"

Mike cut her off. "I don't want to fucking hear it." He turned and walked toward the refrigerator to grab a beer.

"Mike, wait...no. I haven't talked to him in months."

Mike stops, looks at Vanessa, and repeats, "Months!"

"Mike, let me explain. I called him twice while you were still in the hospital. I called to tell him that he and I were over. I want to be with you. I wanted us to be a family."

"Why? 'Cause I got injured? Or was it 'cause you thought you were going to lose me to Em? Did you feel threatened by her since we have a child together?" cried Mike.

"No, it's not that. I realized my actions hurt you. I realized that my indiscretions drove a wedge between us. I'm sorry. You are a good man, a loving husband, and a wonderful father."

"*Was*...I *was* all those things. Now, I'm a broken man, a terrible father, and a fucking idiot of a husband. Get your shit, and get the fuck out!" screamed Mike.

"Mike, wait...please," Vanessa said, crying.

"Did you fucking hear me? Get the fuck out!" Mike yelled and threw his beer across the room.

Vanessa buried her face in her hands and cried.

"I said...get your shit and go!" Mike yelled as he walked back to the bedroom and frantically gathered all of Vanessa's things in his arms and returned to the apartment door.

Vanessa sees Mike with her things and struggles to stay on her feet. "No...Mike...please. Don't do this," pleads Vanessa, violently crying. She reaches for Mike's arm, trying to get him to drop her clothes.

Mike easily breaks her grip, opens the door, and throws her items outside. He turns to Vanessa and says, "Get out, or I will throw you out. Your choice."

A defeated and crying Vanessa looks at Mike. "Babe… please?"

Mike turns away from Vanessa and points toward the parking lot. He watches as Vanessa walks outside and begins to collect her things. A few seconds pass before Mike shuts the door.

Vanessa picks up her belongings and walks to her car. She loads them up and sits in the driver's seat, crying. *What just happened? What could I have done differently?* She sits for a few minutes, waiting, hoping that Mike will come out and ask her to stay.

Ten minutes pass, but he does not. She starts her car and makes the long drive back to her parents' house.

Inside, Mike drops to his knees and begins to bawl. *What is wrong with me? Will I ever be normal again? Why can't I just be sane?* Mike curls into the fetal position, sobbing and asking the same questions over and over again.

About fifteen minutes pass before Mike gets up and walks to the kitchen counter and clutches his pills. He walks over to the refrigerator and grabs another beer. Mike throws the pills to the back of his mouth and swallows them down with the aid of the ice-cold beer.

I don't want to feel a thing, he thinks to himself and grabs another beer…then another…and another…until he has drunk an entire six-pack in a few short minutes.

Mike walks to the couch, plops down on it, and starts to pass out.

A loud bang on the apartment door jolts Mike awake. He gets up and stumbles to the door. "Who is it?" he shouts.

"Sir, it's the police. We got called about a disturbance," shouted a man from the other side of the door. "Could you open up, please," the same voice called out.

"Are you the real police or the wanna-be police?"

"Sir, we are the real police. Now, could you please open up?" said the man's voice.

Mike opens the door and sees two Military Police officers standing on his doorstep.

"I thought you said you were the real police."

"Sir, we got a call about a domestic disturbance. Are you alone?"

"Bro, I'm never alone. I have the memories of my dead friends always with me."

"Sir, do you mind if we come in and take a look around?" asked the second officer.

"Sure, I have nothing to hide. I must warn you though"—the officers look at Mike with their hands on their sidearms—"I don't have any doughnuts, if that's what you're looking for."

The officers look at Mike and then at each other. One stays at the door with Mike, while the other walks into the apartment to look around.

A few minutes pass, and the officer comes back to the door. "We're good here," he says.

"Okay, sir, we are gonna need you to keep it down," the first officer said.

"Yes, sir," Mike says, snapping to attention and sarcastically saluting the officers. The two officers leave Mike's apartment, and Mike forcefully shuts the door behind them. Then he plops back on the couch with a beer in his hand and passes out.

Chapter 33

A week had passed since Mike had last seen or talked to Vanessa. He spent most of the week in a drunken state, barely remembering what day it was.

Mike looks at his calendar. *Fuck, I have a few days left in the Army.*

Mike gets up, lays out an old uniform on the bed, and stands looking at it. A flood of memories fill Mike's mind. He looks over his uniform the way he has done many times in the past. The old, faded uniform is another reminder of the man he once was.

Mike walks to the bathroom and stares in the mirror. He examines his face. His eyes are sunken in. His cheekbones jump off his face like the peaks of the Himalayas. The beard on his face is bushy and wiry. He stands there, desperately trying to find the man he once was.

Mike grabs the straight razor lying to the side of his sink and brings it up to his neck. He takes it and presses the blade into his neck, right over his jugular. A moment passes before he puts the razor down and grabs the shaving cream to lather his forgotten face.

Mike grabs the razor again and begins to shave; with each stroke of the blade, more of his altered image is revealed. After all of his facial hair is gone, Mike stares at the man that he is now. His eyes, once full of life and love, now are cold and black. His smile, which once could light up a room, is gone, replaced by a detached stare.

Mike washes the remnants of shaving cream from his face. *God, what have I become?*

He walks out of the bathroom and sits on the bed to put on his old uniform. He slides into his pants, puts on his boots, and then stands up to adjust his pants. Mike wrenches on his belt to keep his pants from falling. He throws on his brown undershirt before putting on his uniform top.

Mike looks at his reflection in the mirrored closet door. *I look like a kid in his daddy's uniform.* Mike shakes his head at the sad sight. After examining himself for a few minutes more, he walks to the kitchen to take more pills to take the edge off his pain.

Mike grabs a manila folder from the edge of the kitchen table, walks to the door, takes a look around, and leaves the apartment. He makes his way to the parking lot, gets in his car, and drives to the main post to begin his long and arduous process of leaving the only employment he has known for most of his adult life.

The day was spent in a blur of briefing, classes, and appointments. Mike tried his best to pay attention to all the information he was being given, but the reality that he was finally going to be out of the Army kept him in a state of shock.

Mike drove all over the Army base, getting signatures or stamps. Each location shared similar qualities. An old, retired veteran with a superiority complex seemed to be working each front desk; their specialty seemed to be making life more difficult than it needed to be.

For Mike, it seemed that time dragged during this process, while the rest of the world seemed to be running at full speed. At each place Mike stopped during his clearing process, he was met with unique problems. "You have to go to this office first," "Until then, I can't help you," "Oh, you don't have this form," "I can't help you," and even "Well, back in my day, we didn't have these soft snowflakes."

The entire process drained Mike both mentally and physically. Mike finally made it back to his apartment around four that afternoon. He walked in, took a seat on the couch, and tried to process the events of the day. *The fuck happen today?*

Mike removes his uniform and throws it in the corner of the living room. He gets up and goes to the kitchen to grab a beer. Mike shuts the fridge door and goes to the counter to grab his pain medication. *Is this what my life has come to? Is this all that I am?*

Mike goes back to the couch to sit down. He sips his beer and stares at the wall. Mike opens his phone and searches through his music until he finds the song that fit his mood.

As he listens, Mike starts thinking about how things ended with Vanessa. *Should I give her a chance to explain? Did I overreact? Was I wrong?*

Mike's doubts start to anger him. *No, she was wrong. She fucking lied to me. She told me that it was over. And this fucking guy is calling her. And to think that I ended things with Em.*

Thinking about Em calms Mike. He gets up to grab another beer, then returns to the couch. *My sweet Em. I can only imagine how heartbroken she is. She is taking care of her sick mom and our child alone. I was such an asshole toward her.*

Focusing on his actions and how he treated Em infuriates Mike. *How could he act that way to someone he loved so much?* Mike begins to weep from the emotional stress. The pain from his broken heart and shattered soul is unbearable. This pain is new and raw; it is something he has never felt before.

Mike gets up, walks to the fridge, and goes to pull out another beer. *Fuck, I went through the twelve-pack already.* Mike opens the kitchen cabinet and grabs the bottle of 1800 Tequila Blanco. *Well, it looks like it's just you and me,* thinks Mike as he opens the bottle, presses it to his lips, and takes a huge gulp.

Mike measured the time by how much liquor was in the bottle. He could barely keep his eyes open as he tried to look at the clock on the stove—one thirty. *Fuck, I need to go to bed. Tomorrow's another fun-filled day of being treated like a piece of shit.*

Mike tries to stand up from the kitchen table and falls flat on his face. He laughs as he staggers back to his feet and walks toward his bedroom. Mike stops at the kitchen counter, pops open his bottles of pills, and swallows a handful of them.

Walking down the hallway, Mike leans on the wall, keeping himself upright until he gets to his bedroom. Mike heads to the bathroom to brush his teeth. He reaches for his toothbrush and knocks over all the toiletries. He laughs again before picking up the toiletries and attempting to put them back in order. Still laughing, Mike looks in the mirror. He stares himself in the eye...and slowly stops laughing.

"Fuck you," Mike shouts at his reflection. "Fuck you, you piece of shit. I hate you." Mike shouts louder, "I hate you!" Screaming louder and grabbing the straight razor, he yells, "I fucking hate you!" With tears in his eyes, Mike pushes the blade against his throat. "You pussy motherfucker! No one will miss you, you piece of shit!"

Mike's hands shake violently. A small drop of blood peeks from under the razor blade and oozes down Mike's throat. He drops to his knees and rushes to grab the toilet before he retches until the actual vomiting begins.

After Mike has regurgitated the full contents of his stomach, he slowly gets to his feet. But the room starts spinning, and he falls to the floor.

Chapter 34

Mike drops to his knees in the middle of a firefight. He looks around and sees his platoon returning fire on a house filled with insurgents. He tries to return fire, but can't find his weapon. In the distance, he hears a familiar voice.

"Mike! Mike! Save me!" a voice cries out, but Mike can barely make out the person calling his name. "Mike, how could you? Please come to me!" the voice calls out.

Mike runs frantically, trying to find the person calling his name. After searching for a few minutes, Mike finally spots Em across the street from his position. "Em!" he screams. "Em! I'm coming." Mike turns to the soldier next to him, points in the direction of Em, and shouts, "Give me cover fire!"

Mike waits until the soldier starts firing his squad automatic machine gun; then he takes off running. Mike sprints a zigzag pattern in short bursts. I'm up. He sees me. I'm down. *Mike hits the ground as he mumbles the word* down.

Rolling to his left Mike pops up and takes off running again. I'm up. He sees me. I'm down. *Mike drops again on the last word; then he rolls to the right before popping back up again. Mike repeats this process until he is about twenty-five meters from Em.*

Mike begins to smile as Em's face becomes clear.

Em smiles back at him.

Then, a loud whistle overhead…

"Mike! Get down!" Em screams as fear grips her face.

Mike reaches out and tries to grab Em.

The whistle gets louder and louder…

A flash of light from an explosion…

A thunderous boom.

Mike feels the heat from the blast. "Eeeeeeemmmm!" he screams.

* * *

Mike wakes up on the bathroom floor. *What the fuck?* Mike struggles to get to his knees. He reaches for the bathtub's edge to help him get up. Mike sits on the side of the tub. He rubs his head and tries to regain his bearings.

Fuck, what time is it? Mike looks at his watch. *Motherfuck—eleven thirty.* His heart drops because he has to be at a behavioral-health appointment. Mike hurries to his feet and starts to get ready. In only a few minutes, Mike shaves, brushes his teeth, dons his uniform, and is out the door.

Mike arrives at his appointment and checks in. He takes a seat behind two soldiers who are still in training and waiting to be called. Mike takes a drink from his Monster, trying to nurse his headache.

"Yeah, man, I'm trying to get out," one soldier tells the other.

"How are you going to do that?" asks the other.

"Oh, it's easy. I'm just going to tell them that I can't handle being in the Army, and I'm thinking about hurting myself," the first soldier responds.

"Will that really work?" asks the second soldier.

"Yeah, man, I had a buddy that was just discharged for saying the same thing, and he got all his benefits. They medically retired him with one hundred percent disability. It's a way to get all the benefits and not really have to be in the Army."

Hearing these two soldiers talk about cheating the system makes Mike's blood boil. *Here are these two fuck-sticks, trying to game the system to get out, and I'm trying to stay in.*

The two soldiers continued to talk about what to say to get medically discharged. After a few minutes of hearing the soldiers speak, Mike had had enough. He stood up and walked in front of them. "You two are fucking pieces of shit."

The first soldier looks confusedly at Mike.

"You don't want to do the time and put in the effort, that's fine. But lying to get all your benefits is what makes you lower than a fucking roach's nut sac."

The second soldier responds, "Sit down, Grandpa. Don't be mad 'cause we are smart enough to not end up like you."

Mike closed his eyes and counted to three. When the soldiers started laughing at him, Mike opened his eyes and grabbed both the soldiers by their throats. "Look here, you punk motherfuckers"—Mike brought both of them close to his face—"if you go and talk to your counselor and lie to be discharged, I will find out where you live, and I will fucking murder your whole fucking family." Mike reached into their shirts and pulled off their dog tags. "Private Smith and Private Jones, now you have something traumatizing to tell them."

"Sergeant First Class Perez," a voice called out, "the counselor will see you now."

Mike looks at the young woman who called his name. "I'm here," he answered as he made his way to the door.

Mike was escorted down a long hallway and seated in a small room with an oversize wooden desk. Sitting at the desk was a pale man in a light-blue shirt. The man didn't even look up.

"So, Sergeant First Class Perez, looks like you are here to be cleared for retirement. Are you having any night-mares? Or being hypervigilant?" asked the pale man.

"Nope."

"How about excessive drinking or drug use?"

"Nope, I don't really drink."

"It looks like you were involved in a traumatic injury. How are you doing with that? Any flashbacks about it?"

"No, sir. I am doing just fine. The only thing I really have is some pain, but, other than that, I'm pretty much good from my injury."

"Any angry outbursts or feelings of aggression?"

"Oh no, sir. I am as calm as can be."

"Okay, Sergeant First Class Perez, looks like you are good to go. I'll sign off on your paperwork, and we can get you outta here," said the man as he finally looked up at Mike. The man reached out his hand for Mike's discharge paperwork so that he could sign them. He scribbled on it and then handed it back to Mike.

Mike gets up and makes his way to the door. "Thank you," he says as he walks out. *Worthless piece of shit,* he thinks.

Making his way down the hall, he sees one of the soldiers from the lobby. Mike stares at him. "Remember what I told you," says Mike as they pass each other.

Mike made his way to the car and headed to his final appointment in the Army. A mixture of anger, frustration, betrayal, and hatred floods Mike as he pulls into the parking lot of the out-processing center. He sits in the parking lot, gripping the steering wheel until his knuckles turn white.

After all my years of service, it comes down to this. A single tear crawls down his cheek, and he sniffles a bit. Mike clears his throat, reaches over to the passenger's side, grabs his clearing papers, and looks himself in the rearview mirror. *Let's get this over with.*

Mike opens the car door, his papers in hand, and crosses the street to the out-processing center. He looks at the directory to find out where he has to go and heads to the stairwell to go to the second floor. With each step he takes, Mike's heart races faster and faster. By the time he makes it to the second floor, his palms are dripping wet. He opens the stairwell door and walks down the hallway to the last door on the left.

I can't believe this is real. Holy fucking shit. This has to be a fucking dream. What am I going to do next? As far back as I can remember, the military is all I've ever known.

Mike enters the office and signs in; then he takes a seat in the waiting room. He looks around the waiting room and sees that it is mostly filled with young soldiers. Seeing all of them waiting to be discharged enraged Mike. *All these fucking quitters. Fucking pieces of shit. Can't even commit to a few years.*

About ten minutes pass before Mike is called to the back. He takes a seat in front of an old man in a little cubicle. Mike looks around and sees that the cubicle is littered with the man's military awards, pictures of his family, and drawings that appear to be from a little kid.

"Sergeant First Class Perez, welcome. Let me see your paperwork," said the man.

Mike hands him the papers and continues to look at the man's cubicle. He sees a retirement certificate that reads, "Retired Command Sergeant Major."

Fuck, I hope he is not an old, grumpy CSM, Mike thinks.

"Mm-hmm," mumbled the man. "All right, Sergeant First Class Perez, looks like everything checks out. Thank you for your service, and good luck on your next endeavors."

Mike looks at the man with an expressionless face. *This is it. It is finally over.* His heart races so fast it feels as if it were skipping beats. Mike clears his throat. "Thank you," he manages to squeak out, choking down his emotions.

The man hands Mike his paperwork.

Mike grabs it as he stands up and turns to walk away. Returning to the car, Mike sits in the driver's seat. He lets out a primal scream and violently beats his steering wheel. After a few minutes, he regains his composure and starts the ignition. Mike wipes the tears from his face and begins his drive back to the apartment.

On the drive home, all Mike thought about was everything he'd lost since he woke up from his coma. He villainized himself, so Em would hate him and move on. Vanessa lied to him and played him for a fool. The kids were deathly afraid of him after his outburst. The guys from his unit were moving on, having their next missions, and living their lives. And the one thing that gave him a sense of purpose—the one thing he was good at and that he knew how to do—was just stripped away from him.

These thoughts festered, and Mike obsessed about them over and over again until he arrived back at the Fisher House. Mike parked and walked toward his apartment's door. From a distance, he could see a piece of paper taped to it.

The fuck is this now?

Standing in front of the door, Mike reads, "Sergeant First Class Perez, please see the front office. Signed, Management."

Motherfuck! What the fuck now?

Mike tears down the note, crumples it up, and throws it on the ground. He enters the apartment to change out of his uniform before heading to the manager's office.

Entering the lobby of the Fisher House, Mike sees a young man at the desk. "Hey, I had a note to come see the office," Mike said as he approached the desk.

"Sergeant First Class Perez?" asked the young man.

"No, it's just Mr. Perez now."

"Oh, I apologize, sir. One moment while I get the manager."

Mike waited until the manager arrived.

"Sergeant First Class Perez, can you come with me?" says a portly, older woman.

Mike follows her down a short hallway to her office.

"Please have a seat." After he had done so, she continued, "It has come to my attention that your care here has concluded and that you are now no longer in the service. I must inform you that since you are no longer receiving care, and no longer in the service, you can no longer stay at our facility."

Mike felt his stomach drop. "So what the fuck am I supposed to do? Pack up all my shit today and fucking live in my car?"

"Oh no, sir. We would not do that. You have ten days to find a place to stay. We are not heartless, sir. We just have other service members that also need our facilities."

Mike snapped back, "Fine, I'll be out before the ten days are up."

"I apologize for any inconvenience, Sergeant First Class Perez. And I want to thank you for your service."

Mike gets up to leave and mutters, "Yeah, thanks… or whatever," as he walks out.

Mike returns to his room and slams the door behind him. *Holy fuck, can this day get any fucking worse?*

Mike walks over to his kitchen counter, grabs a handful of pills, and chokes them down. Then he walks to the fridge, grabs a can of beer, opens it up, and takes a huge swig from it. Mike walks to his kitchen table and sits down, staring at the floor. He takes another big swig of beer…and then another.

Mike repeats this cycle for a few hours. Lost in his own thoughts. Thinking about everything he's lost. Everything that was taken from him.

Finally, Mike looks at his watch. *Fuck, it's seven o'clock. I should go get some food.* He grabs his keys and stumbles to his car.

The rest of the night is a blur of bars and strip clubs…

Mike finds himself walking down the white center line of a road. *I am so done.* Mike stops walking and just stands in the middle of the road. *C'mon, fucking hit me. C'mon, you cocksucking motherfucker, hit me,* Mike thinks to himself as headlights in the distance get closer.

The driver of the car presses on the horn. As the car gets closer and closer, the horn gets louder and louder.

Mike closes his eyes, stands upright with his arms outstretched, and waits for death…

At the last minute, the car swerves, narrowly missing Mike.

He opens his eyes and drops to his knees, sobbing. "Why God? Why? Make all this stop!" Mike throws up two middle fingers to the sky. "Fuck you, God! Fuck you!" he screams at the top of his lungs. "Fuck you."

Mike walks over to a bench and sits down. "Fuck me. I can't do this anymore. Fuck me." He digs into his pocket and pulls out his cell phone. Closing one eye, trying to read the screen, he scrolls down until he finds a number.

Mike texts the number: *911. Help me.*

He shares his location, then puts his phone away, and passes out on the bench.

* * *

About three hours later, Mike is awakened by someone grabbing him under his shoulders.

"C'mon, bud, I got you. C'mon, get on your feet, brother," Carson said as he helped Mike get to his feet.

"It's time, man. I'm calling in that favor," Mike said, slurring his words.

"What? What favor?"

"The one that would help me end this shit. I can't do this shit anymore," Mike blurted out.

Carson looks at Mike with a confused look.

"Take me home, brother. I need to end this. I can't fucking take it."

Carson managed to drag Mike to the car and pour him into the back seat. Carson shut the car door, walked to the driver's side, got in, and headed to Mike's apartment.

"I'm done...I'm done...I'm done. You promised brother. You promised," Mike kept repeating.

Carson arrived at the apartment, hoisted Mike onto his shoulders using a fireman's carry, and hauled Mike to the door. After opening it, Carson walked to the bedroom and threw Mike on his bed. He took off Mike's shoes and tucked him into bed.

Then Carson walked into the living room and plopped on the couch to get some rest.

Chapter 35

Seven years later...

Mike wakes up and sits on the edge of the bed. The cold air makes Mike's body throb. He rubs his knees and slowly stands up. The wooden floor creaks underneath his weight as he walks to the kitchen, where he glances at a bottle of pills on the countertop.

Mike reaches toward the bottle, but grabs the bag of coffee next to it instead. He turns on the water, fills a coffee mug, and pours it into the water reservoir of the coffee maker. He does this several times before putting three mounded scoops of coffee into the filter and turning the coffee maker on.

As the coffee is brewing, Mike walks back to the bedroom and puts on a few layers of clothes. He sits back down on the bed and puts on his running shoes. Mike catches his reflection in the mirror.

It's gonna be a good day, he thinks to himself as he gives his reflection a big smile.

Mike gets up, walks to the outside door, and goes outside. The brisk mountain air sends a cold chill through his body. He brings his hands to his face and blows into them. His breath fogs in front of him.

Let's do this. Mike hits Play on his phone and loud rock music starts playing.

Mike trots down the wooden stairs of the log cabin and starts a light jog down the snow-covered, gravel driveway. He reaches the end of the driveway and turns left on the road to start his morning run. He runs down the winding road for four miles before turning around and running back to the cabin.

He makes his way back up the driveway and walks up the gravel path to the cabin. Mike enters the cabin, makes his way to the wooden stove, and throws a few logs in it to warm up the house.

Mike walks to the bathroom and strips down to take a shower. He turns on the hot water and steps in. The hot water on Mike's body feels good on his sore muscles. He stands in the shower and lets the hot water drench every fiber of his being.

Stepping out of the shower, Mike reaches for a towel and dries off. With the towel, he wipes the mirror. He stares at his body, amazed at the transformation. He was no longer the weak, sickly man he was in the hospital. Mike can see his muscular body is slowly returning. He turns to look at his right side.

Mike examines his body and rubs his hands over the scars that still pit his skin. He puts on his clothes and walks to the kitchen to pour himself a big mug of coffee. Walking outside, he takes a seat on a wooden chair on the cabin's deck. Mike props his feet up and slowly sips his coffee.

Mike stares off in the distance until something catches his eye. He focuses and analyzes it, finally making out that it is a vehicle. He stands up and follows the vehicle with his eyes.

Fuck, this can't be good.

Mike watches as the vehicle gets close enough to make out the make.

I know that truck. If they are coming here, then this isn't good.

Mike stared as the Toyota Tundra slowed down in front of his driveway and turned onto the gravel road leading to his cabin. Mike sips his coffee as the truck comes to a stop a few feet from the base of his stairs.

Carson and Jose get out of the truck and start walking toward Mike.

"What's wrong, guys?"

Carson looks at Jose, waiting for him to say something.

"Mike…it's Papi…" Jose says with a grave look on his face. "His cancer came back. Can we go inside and talk?"

Mike stares at Jose and Carson for a few moments; then he looks down at the ground.

"C'mon in, guys. The coffee's still hot," Mike finally says as he turns and heads inside.

Jose walks up the stairs, following Mike.

Carson brings up the rear. Before entering the house, he turns and looks at the scenery. After taking a deep breath and letting out a big sigh, Carson walks in the cabin and closes the door.